MW01041498

dancing with His Heart

katherine warwick

Grove Creek Publishing

This is a work of ficiton. Names, characters, places and incidents are either a product of the author's imagination of are used fictitiously, and any resemblance ot actual persons, living or dead, business establishments, events or locales is entirely coincidental.

A Grove Creek Publishing Book / published by arrangement with the author

DANCING WITH HIS HEART
Printing History

Grove Creek Publishing edition / June 2006

Cover artwork by Jennifer Johnson.
Book Design by Julia Lloyd.

ISBN: 1-933963-98-0

Printed in the United States of America

To the inspiring talent at *Center Stage*,
especially Rick Robinson
for sharing his passionate productions.

one

The woman could move. Creamy skin gleamed with the
sheen of her sweat. Slashes of crimson sequins barely covered
her breasts, wrapped like a greedy fist around her tiny waist.
Her upper thighs shone temptingly beneath the whisper of a
sheer red skirt. As if her body yearned to be free of even the
necessary confinement of the costume, she spun, writhed, and
twisted to the demands of the pounding Latin beat.

And Alex was her prisoner.

He stood with his back against the wall, his heart
thudding to the sensual tune. He'd come in too late to garner a
seat. But he couldn't sit if he wanted to. His blood roared at the
very sight of her.

She taunted with fluid arms that beckoned, whipped,
then imprisoned. Her face, deceptively angelic, lured with
the smile of promise – a promise only bestowed when she
permitted. With her hips she swung, undulating in a rabid heat
that shot waves of desire from his mouth to his belly.

He started to sweat.

Lauren. That body of hers had tempted him from the
very beginning, planting a vision of liquid fire in his head that
burned with unquenchable flames as the years passed.

He meant to feel that flame for himself now, even if he
knew he'd get burned.

Desire moved him through the crowd. He didn't even excuse himself to those standing in his way, he just shouldered past them, his eyes fixed on her, dancing.

The music changed. From a sultry Latin beat it became quick and snappy. No longer did those long, lovely limbs summon and captivate. The jive took Lauren and her partner into a joyful celebration, the final dance of the five Latin dances of love.

Because of Lauren, Alex knew the difference between rumba and samba. He'd learned that the five Latin dances told a story, taking the audience through flirtatious cha-cha through culmination in jive.

Alex stood at the hem of the dance floor, in the fringe of light for an unadulterated view, hoping she would see him.

Whether or not she recognized him, he didn't know. The years made him a man, her a woman, a fact he was more than anxious to remind her of when he finally got his hands on her.

Alex felt a smile coming. Their relationship wasn't even flirtatious; he knew it would be more accurate in fact to call it distant. That was why he was there – to change it.

Because a healthy dose of admiration sung through his veins, there was more to his plan than just saying hello. Getting reacquainted was only the beginning. She needed him, a fact he was sure she'd fight. He expected that. Indeed, one of the reasons he was drawn to her was the chemistry that lit his system whenever the two of them were face-to-face. Two brush fires out of control. From day one, he'd been intrigued by her, aloof, sassy, beautiful. Time may have kept him a stranger, but it hadn't sequestered his need to keep an eye on where life had taken her.

And so he was there, for reasons both of them would

come to accept as inevitable.

When Lauren finished dancing, Alex's body was free to sigh. Chad, her partner and Alex's friend, led her off stage. Alex's gaze didn't leave them until they disappeared off deck behind long, blue drapes.

The floor filled with other competitors, these in black tuxedos and pastel dresses elegantly spinning to the light and classical music of the Viennese waltz. Having seen all he came to see, Alex made his way to one of the tables sitting at the edge of the dance floor where Chad had told him to meet so the three of them could talk.

Like a teenager, his stomach fluttered with butterflies. Lauren. It was a reaction he was accustomed to whenever he neared her – he shouldn't be surprised. Soon that heat would smolder and skip, lighting into something that had consumed him all these years. And still did, even now.

* * *

Alex Saunders. It seemed unreal to hear his name. And now Lauren's heart thumped out of control. Her palms sweat around the paper program in her hands. Her head craned, her eyes darted through the crowd to see if she could find him – not that she wanted him to see her.

Years had helped her forget him – that and the fact that he had gone off to Princeton on his family money after high school.

Now, she couldn't believe what Chad just told her.

"No way would Alex Saunders sponsor us," she said. Chad, her new dance partner, led her through the boisterous crowd to the table they had reserved on the dance floor to observe the competition.

"Yes. He wants us." Chad pulled out a chair. Lauren sat, looking through the crowd for that tall lanky form and beacon of black hair belonging to Alex. "He's totally excited about it."

Lauren's stomach twisted. "Are you sure he knows I'm your partner?"

"He knows." Chad watched couples from the audience dance in the open session of the evening's events. It was the only time the audience participated, with the exception of expected cheering for their favorite couple. "In fact, he approached me about it."

A knot of suspicion formed in Lauren's stomach. Alex Saunders, proverbial rich man, philanthropist and resident playboy seeking her out? There was only one reason for such a contradictory act, and her stomach churned at the thought.

Catching the eye of another competitor mulling through the crowd, she waved and smiled. Lauren wouldn't allow Alex's presence to dampen her evening. She and Chad had done their guest performance with perfection; the standing ovation they received was satisfying. Besides, it had been years since those warring and tumultuous days of high school. She and Alex were adults now. Things change. People change.

"Well. It's been a long time." The voice behind her had deepened, but the tight mischievousness was still there.

Lauren turned in her chair and looked up.

His eyes sparkled like black sky.

Chad was up in a flash, extending a hand to shake. "Dude, you made it."

Alex spared Chad a glance, but his eyes remained tight with Lauren's. "I wouldn't miss it. Lauren Peay. It's been a while, hasn't it?" He extended a well-groomed hand she merely glanced at, and she didn't bother rising from her chair.

"My, this is a surprise. I didn't think I'd ever see you again." A halo of black hair shocked drama to cheeks and facial planes thinned with maturity. He'd worn his hair short back in high school. Now it hung in loose tangles just at his collar, framing his face with the chic perfection of a celebrity.

Lauren's gaze moved back out over the dancers.

"Disappointed?" Alex asked.

Curious was more like it. But Lauren kept the smile on her face and waved at a friend across the dance floor as she waited for Alex to get the cue that she was not going to touch him.

Chad pulled out a chair on Lauren's right for Alex then planted himself on her left. Purposefully, Alex didn't sit, and Lauren fought the natural urge to see why.

She didn't like that he remained standing, looking down at her. "You haven't changed a bit."

He sat then, his elegantly dressed form stretching out. The tanned glow of his skin was rich against his navy dress jacket and white shirt. Pearl-grey slacks clung to smooth thighs before draping to his polished leather shoes.

His legs crossed and one arm rested behind her on the back of her chair, the other poised importantly on the tabletop. "Still as sassy as you always were."

And proud of it, she thought, but only sent him a pleasant nod. Lauren looked at his lips, pulled back in the mocking smile she remembered so well. The white of his teeth glittered off his ivory shirt, open at the throat. "Since when were you interested in ballroom dance?" Lauren asked.

Alex's dark eyes twinkled. "I've been keeping my eye on it for a long time."

The look shot fire right through her. She shifted in her chair, turning her gaze to the dancers. She noticed whispers and stares from those around them, angled at the single playboy sitting at their table.

Everyone knew Alex Saunders – knew all about the Saunders money establishing most anything of real value in Utah. Long, generous and controlling fingers that spread from government to vast real estate holdings to cultural puppet strings like art, well-chosen museum donations. And ballroom dance competitions.

Chad tapped his wiry leg to the cha-cha beat. "I had no idea you two knew each other before. It's, like, such a small world, isn't it?"

Alex's smile deepened with pleasure. "A very small world. So, how've you been, Lauren? You look…well, you've only gotten more beautiful, if that's possible. And that performance was…perfect."

Lauren bit back a snort. He probably honed those lines on women he skipped through at Princeton. She couldn't thank him for the compliment, sure it wasn't sincere, so she flashed him a smile just as insincere, then looked back over the dance floor. "Thanks."

Alex leaned forward, amused. "I'm getting a distinctly hostile vibe from you."

"Hostile? You and me?" She let out a fluttering laugh meant to cover up the confusion going on inside of her. What did he really want?

Chad laughed, uncomfortable with the situation. "So, you guys – uh – how did you know each other?"

"We went to junior high and high school together," Alex said.

"We weren't friends." Lauren always told it like it was. "He hated me, actually."

Chad's light brows shot up, his forced smile flattened. "Seriously?"

Lauren enjoyed that Alex shifted in the chair next to her then. Maybe she could make him itchy enough that he'd take this ridiculous idea of sponsoring them and shove it in the tailpipe of whatever fancy car he drove.

"Lauren's exaggerating," Alex finally said with a politician's calm. The corner of his jaw knotted as he looked at her. "And that was a long time ago, wasn't it?"

The inscrutable tone of his voice left her totally confused. Her faint hope that time had changed them both was now in question.

The dance floor filled with the first heat of junior Latin competitors and Lauren smiled at them in an effort to ignore the discomfort she felt inside. She was there to enjoy herself, and thinking about the mess Chad had created for them by bringing Alex into their partnership ruined one of few respites she allowed herself.

The emcee announced the numbers of the couples competing, as pairs stood ready on deck in a colorful confetti of costumes. The boys wore black, fitted slacks, their shirts cut to the navel for the sensuous Latin moves. Hair was practically slicked back to enable both audience and judge to witness animated expressions of love and desire. Girls' dresses ranged from flirty to fluffy, sensuous to sassy in every bright color of the rainbow.

Music swirled in the air. Lauren noticed Alex tapping his left hand on the royal blue tablecloth. His ring finger was naked. She'd heard that he wasn't married. Figures, she thought, he'd play as long as he could. Use a woman up then throw her out – his mentality was that of a four-year-old plowing through a toy box.

So he'd gone to Princeton and graduated in Law. As far as she knew, he'd not stepped one foot in a courtroom and that degree was nothing more than a paper pacifier for over-indulgent parents who probably thought the sun rose and the moon circled in their son's promises of someday.

"I was glad to hear you were still dancing," Alex told her, forcing her into conversation.

"It's something I love to do." It hadn't been easy, her personal circumstances as they were, but she refused to let anything keep her from pursuing her dreams. And it had saved her in too many ways to count, a tender fact she guarded.

When the first round of competition ended, she applauded with everyone else, sitting forward so that she would not see Alex in her peripheral vision.

"These kids are really good." In spite of her efforts to distance herself, he leaned closer, and his hot whisper sent an unexpected tingle down her neck. "You were good – just like that." He stayed close. Close enough so she could smell him – rich and spicy. "I remember it well."

Because she enjoyed his nearness, she was angry with herself. "Your memory is selective. How convenient for you." Elbows on the table, she rested her chin on clasped fingers. "Keeps the light that shines on our past from reflecting the dark truth, doesn't it?"

"It seems we have some things to talk about."

"I'm here to support the competition."

"That's why I'm here."

"Chad told me you were coming to talk about

sponsoring us. Which is the real reason you're here?"

Purposefully he brushed his lips to her ear. "If you want to talk about this, let's go outside where we can have some privacy."

"Still luring girls into parking lots? No thanks. I try not to repeat my mistakes."

He was so near she saw the slightest flare of his nostrils. But it was the way his eyes blackened with old treachery that caused her an unwanted shiver. He looked as if he might combust from the inside out, as if every cell was holding back. Suddenly he stood, his male presence towering over her.

"You leaving us?" Chad was up on his feet. "I thought we were going to discuss the arrangement."

"There is no arrangement." Lauren kept her expression flat as she looked up at Alex. "Good evening, Mr. Saunders." Then she turned to the dancers, satisfaction rifling through every inch of her.

"We'll be in touch." Alex shook Chad's hand then moved into Lauren's line of vision. He lingered there just long enough to send a shot of panic through Lauren, not sure what he would do next. She couldn't believe she was doing it again – taunting her nemesis.

"As always, a pleasure, Lauren." His tone was artificially mild.

When the spicy scent of him finally vanished, she nearly crumpled there at the table. What had gotten into her? Just like that she had reverted to the snippy, defensive girl he had tormented with such obvious pleasure.

Chad sat with a disgruntled thud. "That went well."

Lauren kept a controlled facade out over the dancers. "There isn't going to be a sponsorship."

"He was trying to be cordial. You were the one throwing spears."

"You don't know him like I do, Chad." This was where their age difference bothered her. Chad may not look six years her junior, and he certainly danced her equal, but socially, he stumbled out of step behind her.

"He's a friend of mine, Lauren. And you weren't trying at all here. How do you expect us to land a primo situation like this again? I'm telling you, there's nobody—"

"I know, I know." It was a dancer's dream. Very few couples landed sponsors with the resources, name and power of a man like Alex. But she could only envision scenes of subjugation when she pictured their partnership under his dominant hand.

"Just think about it," Chad continued as the next heat began. Twelve couples were trimmed down to six. "He can get us Reuben La Bate."

Lauren looked at him as if he dangled an eight-carat diamond in front of her eyes. "He's retired."

Chad shook his head, a smile of conquest cracking his lips. "Not for a price."

"I heard through the grapevine he's had enough."

"Not the way Alex explained it to me. He told me he'd get the very best for us – no matter the cost."

Alex's high-handedness infuriated Lauren more. "Of course, he thinks money can buy anything."

"Well, can't it?"

It can't buy me, Lauren thought. She'd made it alone for two years now and the price had been too much to shackle her future to one of Alex Saunders' gabardine pant legs. But the competitor inside left her mind watering with the idea of winning, of finally getting her feet out of financial mud and making some progress in any direction, be it the world of dance or in her personal life. A flash of Alex's face quickly replaced the vision. Whether she liked it or not, she was confused and intrigued that Alex suddenly wanted something that would involve her. Impossible, she thought, working to clear her head of his sparkling eyes. But she couldn't. They glittered there, dark and mystifying, causing her nerves to both tingle and twitch.

two

As Lauren drove home, she didn't think about the excitement of the competition or any of the costumes that had caught her eye. She didn't muse over tricky step combinations she'd seen, something she was prone to do after a comp.

She couldn't get Alex's face out of her mind.

She hated Alex Saunders, and her mind wandered back to that night when things between them had changed.

To date, it was her most horrifying night, and just thinking about what almost happened in that parking lot made her shudder. It would be reckless of her to even entertain joining forces with Alex. She wouldn't do it.

It was after ten when Lauren finally pulled her 1995 Toyota Camry into the driveway of her small home. The car needed a new set of tires and something rattled in the engine, but she drove with her fingers crossed that she'd have more time before it finally broke down.

What a little extra money could do for her right now. Forget about supporting Rebekah's special needs – that would be a lifetime effort of gargantuan proportions. As a single mom she tried not to think about all of the necessities in raising a handicapped child, or she found herself close to despair. Just having enough money to fix the occasional clogged shower would be a luxury at this point.

Thoughts of an economic nature wearied her, and she made herself think about the dancing she'd seen at the competition to cushion her dragging spirits before she went inside. As much as she looked forward with a mother's tender heart to seeing her daughter, the sight often carried the bittersweet combination of heartache and joy.

The caregiver, Aubrey, usually did her homework after putting Rebekah to bed.

Lauren expected to find Aubrey at the living room coffee table over a stack of college books. Instead, she heard Aubrey's voice from the hall and felt a slug of concern and irritation. Rebekah was still awake.

It wasn't Aubrey's fault her child wasn't asleep. Rebekah's recent cycle was that of a hamster – awake all night and eating. It didn't matter how Lauren tried to tire her little five-year-old body out, her daughter's internal clock was messed up somehow. Lauren kicked off her shoes and headed to Rebekah's bedroom.

She found her climbing the heavy-duty plastic bookshelf as if she were outside on a jungle gym. Rebekah giggled, babbling in her sweet, high-pitched voice, the voice of an angel lost somewhere but content to be lost. Shadowing her every move was Aubrey, with a smile of patience on her face.

Aubrey's silky blonde hair had been neatly pulled back in a claw when she'd arrived four hours earlier. It hung in tangles now, the claw clinging like a tired climber to a crumbling mountainside.

"Hi." Lauren paused in the door, observing the disaster of Rebekah's bedroom. Books lay on the floor like ticker tape after a parade. Toys Rebekah would probably never play with such as pots, pans, fake food and dolls with all of their accoutrements had been tossed like the inconsequential *things* that they were. The occasional offering of pity by way of gifts a child with autism would have no use for.

"Rough night?" Lauren reached over and picked up a

Barbie doll Peter's mother insisted Rebekah have.

"Girls need dolls, and she's a girl," Peter's mother had stubbornly told her.

Lauren laughed now. Rebekah is a girl with autism – she might as well be from another planet. That was how it felt sometimes trying to understand how her daughter's brain worked.

"I tried to get her to bed." Aubrey blew strings of hair out of her eyes. "But I heard her, came in, and she's been all over the place ever since."

"Maybe she ate something." Lauren went to Rebekah who only briefly looked at her before continuing her desperate and inexplicable climb over the bulky, fat plastic bookshelf.

"I only let her eat what you left for her." Aubrey was well aware of the strict diet Lauren had Rebekah on. It made a marked difference in Rebekah's behavior though there were still unexplainable times. Like now, when she behaved as though twenty monkeys were stuck inside trying to get out.

At last Rebekah was at the top of the bookshelf – a good five feet off the ground. Her eyes were wide, electric, and full of wild mischief, as she stood perfectly confident. She giggled uncontrollably at both Aubrey and Lauren.

"Okay, okay, you did it." Lauren reached for her, knowing the minute her child's feet hit the ground, she would be right back at it like a robot with a loose wire.

Lauren held her on her hip, the thirty-pound five-year-old solid against her body. Instantly, Rebekah squirmed for freedom, her eyes glued to the bookshelf. Lauren just tightened her grip.

"Want me to clean up?" Aubrey bent over, started to clean, but Lauren shook her head.

"Not tonight, I'm bushed. But thanks." She set her arm around the girl's shoulder and the two of them walked back to the living room. "Any exciting news?" Lauren knew Aubrey was dating someone she really liked, and even though she would be devastated to lose the help if Aubrey chose to marry, she cared for her like a sister.

"We're going out tomorrow night, if you don't need me that is."

Lauren shifted the still-wiggling Rebekah who grunted as she leaned and reached toward her bedroom. "Go, Aub. I can't wait to hear about it."

Aubrey's smile was the relief of someone not attached by blood or heart to something permanently shackled. She swung her purse over her shoulder and took Rebekah's reaching arms in her hands to try to get the child's attention.

"Bye, Rebekah. Look at Aubrey, please. Rebekah, look at Aubrey."

For a perfect millisecond, Rebekah went still and looked at Aubrey, and both Lauren and Aubrey smiled with thrill. "Good girl," Aubrey told her. "Say, bye-bye, Aubrey."

Rebekah reached for the bedroom. "Bye, Aub."

"Very good." As with anything verbal and coherent that came from her daughter's mouth, Lauren felt tears start in the back of her eyes considering it a small miracle.

After Aubrey had gone, Lauren turned Rebekah's face to hers so she had to look her in the eye. "Good girl for using your words." Motherly pride had her hugging Rebekah against her, even if she felt her stiffen.

Lauren let her child slip from her arms. Rebekah raced back to her bedroom and the recognizable clunk and thump of her habitual climbing once again began.

Rubbing the back of her neck, Lauren let out a sigh and started turning off lights. She picked up her kitchen timer, a white-bottomed red-topped hen that could keep Rebekah busy for hours as she twisted it just to hear the fast tick of the wind up mechanism inside.

Down the hall was the black fringy tassel of the bell-pull she'd bought at an estate sale. Against her better judgment, Lauren hung the bell pull, having ascribed long ago to the opinion that even though her daughter had a baffling handicap, she would not let it affect how she chose to live her life. If she wanted to purchase something pretty for the house, even if it were fragile, Lauren bought it anyway.

Some days later, she found Rebekah standing on top of her bookshelf dangling the severed fringe over her palm as she stared blankly into nothing.

It was like that with autism, something would catch Rebekah's attention and until she had it, she would go after it with the determination of a rottweiler on the scent of meat. Lauren often wished Rebekah's obsessions would include learning – if she could just stay on task, there would be hope for her tongue to blossom, for her eyes to open to the world around her.

Between her fragile dreams for Rebekah and her lousy run in with Alex, Lauren was besieged with a mood fouler than two-week old diapers. Thank God, Rebekah had finally figured that part out. What a blessing that was, not lifting the legs of a thirty-pound child, cleaning the waste of an adult.

Lauren looked at her drawn, hollowed face in the bathroom mirror. It seemed purple shadows permanently resided under her eyes. She never got enough rest. With Rebekah's unpredictable patterns, her mother antenna lived on high alert, and even the slightest sound jolted her upright in bed with her heart pounding for fear Rebekah had somehow gotten out of the house.

There was something so unfair about the utter vulnerability of a child with autism. Anything could happen to them and they had no voice to defend, reject or even encourage circumstances. It overwhelmed Lauren's sense of right and wrong and completely stretched her maternal drive to protect.

"You look wasted," she told herself in the mirror.

Her dark hair needed highlights. The brown shade once gleamed naturally from the sun. The rich sable color still made the green in her eyes look like shimmering leaves of a tree. She'd always liked her eyes, knew they were one of her best features. Exotic, she'd heard more times than she could count. She laughed wispily now, if she only had a dollar for every time she had been told that she would have four new tires for her car at the very least.

Peter had loved her eyes – once. "I could die there," he used to tell her. She'd thought it was sappy and romantic when she loved him. She didn't know now if he'd ever loved her. Her mind could not understand how you could really love someone yet leave them because the child you created in love was less than perfect.

Divorce papers came soon after, not any great shock to Lauren, but that meant the very long and jagged road of raising their child was hers alone to walk.

She felt the familiar unyielding weight living on her shoulders press more heavily tonight as she went to Rebekah's room. She tried to smile when she saw her baby standing on the top shelf. Rebekah looked at her for the brief second Lauren had grown accustomed to and learned to accept. Deep inside, she took another deep lashing to her already bruised soul. Her beautiful angel would never look her in the eye and say, "I love you, mommy."

As tears rushed to her eyes, Lauren went to her, carrying the faintest hope that her child would see her tears and understand what they meant. But Rebekah's eyes were fixed on something somewhere unseen. Her delicate fingers were engaged in the never ceasing back and forth brushing motion upon her open palm. Lauren wept openly on her tiny shoulder and set her in bed, tucking the blankets and sheets around her. Rebekah's fingers never stopped.

"I love you," Lauren said it anyway, kissing her daughter's cheek, leaving her tears there. At last Rebekah's fingers stopped, but only to wipe the wet from her cheek.

three

There was nothing like music, movement and the exquisite joy that came when you put them together. Dance was the one thing Lauren knew for certain she could lose her frustrations in. Now, readying for her first class, that anxious jitter she always felt returned like a welcome friend.

As children filtered into class, Lauren greeted them with open arms and an encouraging smile, shifting her thoughts to the intrinsic joy of teaching. Most of the children wanted to be there, and a few required creative coaxing in the form of rewards such as hugs or sticks of gum.

Once class was full, she clapped them to attention and the dozen wiggling eight to ten-year-old boys and girls stood like soldiers awaiting their first command.

"Okay, everybody, let's begin by greeting the person next to you the proper way when you want someone to dance with you."

They were paired boy-girl. They turned to each other, extended hands, and shook. Muttered awkward greetings of, "Hello, I'm so-and-so, would you like to dance?" followed.

Lauren smiled. It was going to be a great class.

They didn't fight, they didn't argue and they kept up with her, which she considered a small miracle she would snatch in view of the week she'd had so far.

She demonstrated, encouraged and praised for four hours, never once looking at the clock after each class came and left. Rebekah and her safety were tucked away in the capable hands of Aubrey, who would pick her up from school and take her home.

When her studio, one of eight at Center Stage, cleared of its last tired student and parent, she put on some of her favorite tunes and ran the sweeper across the hardwood floor.

It was her private indulgence, to allow music to pound into her when she was alone. No one could make her bones rubber like vintage Michael Jackson, and she put on *Beat It*. In a moment of jesting, she used the handle as her dance partner and shimmied and dipped and swirled around it.

She enjoyed watching herself in the mirror, pleased with her fluid form and the sensual beauty she worked hard to convey as she moved her body to music. Vanity was a natural extension of a dancer that she would neither deny nor hide. She cared about how she looked. She knew that beauty was made even more potent in combination with her body and what she could do with it. It had gotten to Alex Saunders that night so long ago, and that was something she would never forget.

The way he'd looked at her – as if she were a genie mystically wafting just out of reach that he wanted more than anything but couldn't have. She hadn't known then what the look of desire was. Years and other men taught her how to read the opposite sex. And she didn't know how many women enjoyed even a moment's control over tough and terrible Alex Saunders, but she had. That was worth savoring.

So wrapped up in the delight of past reprisal, she didn't notice the studio door opening until a biting draft tickled her exposed arms, legs and the back of her neck.

She had worn her usual black stretch top cut low in the back and tight everywhere else. Her short black skirt flared when she moved, hung enticingly over her upper thighs when she stood perfectly still, as she was right now.

Alex Saunders was watching her.

She held the broom handle close to her thumping heart and wiped a light mist of perspiration from her forehead, commanding herself to stay calm. Beat It was over, and Michael Jackson was singing sweetly about the lady in his life.

Immediately she crossed to the music and turned it down – not off, that would not be enough background for the awkward silence she anticipated.

"Dancing with brooms?" Alex let the door close behind him. He wore the lightest cream slacks in silky fabric that draped rather than hung, accentuating hard lines and worked muscles. His white shirt was fluid as well, even under his deep chocolate leather jacket. The contrasts made his dark eyes pierce her from across the room.

Being cordial was not an option; she knew what he was here for. Lauren resumed sweeping.

"If you would only let me sponsor you, you could be dancing with Chad instead of that broom."

"I'll be dancing with Chad whether you sponsor us or not." She didn't like that he even remotely dangled a threat.

"Sounds like it might be easier to replace a partner than find a sponsor."

Lauren stopped, looked at him. His head tilted slightly. She wouldn't believe that Chad would end their new partnership just because she wasn't willing to kiss Alex Saunders' manicured hand. Solid partnerships were as hard to come by as multi-millionaires willing to take dancers under their wing.

Deciding that he was just bluffing, she continued to sweep.

"I came in hopes that you would let me talk you into the privilege of sponsoring you," he said.

"I'm flattered, but I'm still declining your offer."

Sliding his hands in his pockets, Alex rocked on his heels with a smile. "You have others you're considering then?"

"No," she said simply. The floor was clean and she set the broom in a corner, then slowly crossed the floor to him. Something in his eyes flashed and she almost stopped in the safety of the center of the room, feeling deceptively yet deliciously lured. But she would not allow him any room to think his presence mattered.

When she was inches away from him, his pupils dilated and she stopped. "I seem to remember what happened to Daniel Webster when he signed his agreement."

The corner of his lip turned up. "You still think I'm the devil, Lauren?"

"The very twisted, carnal, conniver himself."

His gaze didn't move from her face, even as he studied her with inferno-like heat. "I'm not the same person you knew then. I intend to prove that to you."

"Not necessary, because I don't care who you are now." She turned to gather her things, and he hung uncomfortably close like a bee ready to pollinate a flower. His scent had changed, she'd caught that much at the competition – more sophisticated cologne, she presumed, mixed with the natural tang of him. It filtered through her anger and dislike with the ease of exotic incense.

"That disappoints me." He watched her pull on a black sweater, fluff her hair, then move in front of the mirror for a makeup check.

"I imagine that's not a new emotion for you, where I'm

concerned." She reached in her bag for her powder compact. "Your contempt for me was obvious – I find disappointment rather a mild word."

He stood directly behind her right shoulder, looking at her reflection as she blotted away shine. "Your memory has distorted the past into something that, yes, I'll admit, existed." He paused for her reaction but there was none. "But does not exist now."

She started to laugh. "You are so full of it." Then she brought out a tube of deep plum lipstick and slowly spread it across the surface of her lips.

She couldn't believe that his skin flushed. He dipped his dark head for a moment. "You're not going to give me any credit, and that's okay." His eyes met hers again. "You think you knew me back then. If you did, you knew there were three things I couldn't back away from." He positioned himself closer to her, his breath hot on her exposed neck. "A fight, a verbal challenge of any kind, and a woman in distress."

"Even if it's you causing the distress?"

"You're never going to forgive me for saving that pretty little butt of yours that night, are you?"

"You didn't save anything. You talked your friends into cornering me, practically raping me, and then stepped in so that you looked like a hero."

The flash of fury that set his jaw startled her, and she turned around, facing him.

"That was not a set up," he said through teeth. "I would never do something like that – to anyone. Not even a girl I thought I hated."

"There was no *thought* about it, Alex. You most definitely hated me."

He looked more alert when she said his name. His face softened. "I've never heard you say my name before."

Why it mattered, Lauren couldn't imagine. Why she felt a delightful pinch of power baffled her even more. And she had said his name, plenty of times. She'd cursed it, screamed it. In her dreams she'd whispered it.

"You just said you hated me – you admitted it at the competition as well."

He wet his lips. "You want to talk about this now?"

"Actually," she glanced at the clock on the wall, "I don't. I have to get home so my babysitter can get on with her weekend." She started toward the door.

"I'm not through talking to you, Lauren." He stayed on her tail with the determination of a guard dog.

"You have to be, Alex, because I have to go."

His body blocked her hasty exit when they reached the door. "This is important."

Reaching around him, her hand skimmed the side of his leather jacket and she gripped the handle. "No, my child is important. My babysitter and her love life are important." She pulled, but Alex didn't budge.

"You're right," he started, making it clear that he was going nowhere until he said what he wanted to say. "I had… issues with you when we were kids. I don't know." He shrugged but didn't try to smile, to hide the truth, and Lauren found that shockingly pleasant. "It was kid stuff. Stupid. The point is, Chad's a friend of mine, and I know you two need a sponsor."

The puzzle pieces were too skewed for her liking. "How long have you known him?"

"Our families have been friends for years."

"He's never mentioned you."

"Chad's seven years younger than me. The age difference factor might have been an issue."

"More issues for poor Alex. I'm still not buying it." She reached behind him again for the door and again he remained a boulder.

"Don't try to pretend this sponsorship isn't a godsend to you, Lauren. Where else would you two go? Nobody else can offer what I'm offering – unlimited money. Unlimited."

Lauren licked her lips absently. Her mind was already going there, dreaming about the red carpet unrolling Supadance shoes, diamondy gowns, and first class travel to any competition of their choosing. It was the chance of a lifetime, but could she tolerate the hand extended to her?

She looked at Alex's face, deceptively handsome. He smelled too darned good, dressed like a Nordstrom's window mannequin, and that Saunders money was sewn into every piece of his hand-tailored clothing. Clearly she was losing it even considering the alliance. Nothing was that good. She may not have had much, but her self-respect she would never sell, and entering in a contract with Alex was tantamount to sticking a for sale sign on her forehead.

He was as hardheaded as she; that much had not changed about him. A keg of dynamite wouldn't move him from the door. She wondered if something much subtler but just as powerful would.

She reached behind him again for the knob, but this time she pressed her entire body into his. His eyes went wide for a millisecond and the corner of his jaw twitched. Her heart fluttered delightfully, but she worked to control resolve and pressed there into him just long enough to feel him shift slightly. Melting – she hoped. Enough for her to open the door and leave him, slamming it shut in his face.

His firm chin lifted, and those black eyes of his skittered over her face but he still did not move. "You feel better than I remember," his voice was low, the sexy tone of a trombone.

Her knees were embarrassingly close to shaking, so she locked them. He felt like a rock all the way down: hard, strong and just as intense as she remembered. For a moment she wondered what drove that intensity through him. It made her feel like she could be both crushed and consumed, and yet still savor the experience.

For years, he'd used that slick, mean tongue to torment her. He was doing it again, and she was strong enough to take it. But she had ways of tormenting. Letting go of the knob, she reached a hand up, her fingers slowly trailing the lapel of his leather jacket, fingering their way toward his face.

The hollow at the base of his throat thrummed with his quickened pulse, and as her eyes wandered the tight skin of his neck, down where his white shirt was spread open, she had the flash of desire to reach her hand beneath the opening and search for the beat of his heart.

His chest lifted in breath then held. That pleased her. Finally, she was burrowing into a weakness. Her lazy study of him wound its way to his mouth, and she purposefully licked her lips. His throat constricted, and against the full length of her, his body shifted to marble. So tight, she felt her own body tingle wondering if he might burst right there on the spot.

When their eyes finally leveled, it was deliciously satisfying to watch the black struggle going on in him. Alex Saunders may have hated her once, but he wanted her now.

No stranger to the hunger of desire in men, Lauren had never used her power as a woman like this before. But with

Alex, she'd use any weapon necessary, even if it placed her in danger. She'd fought and won before, and she would do it again.

Finally, his chest moved and she heard him breathe. He let out a sigh, moved aside and opened the door for her.

"Consider my offer carefully," he told her, letting her pass.

She only looked at him as she went through the door. Her stride was confident and sure, with just enough swing in her hips to ensure that his mouth still watered, his nerves still ticked. Purposefully, she kept pace in front of him. Her car wasn't far, and he'd parked his sleek, black BMW right next to it. How convenient, she thought, hoping her back view was making his blood roar.

Growing up in front of mirrors she'd learned how she looked from every angle, so when she slipped her key into the lock, she bent over just enough that her backside rounded temptingly. She stole a glance at Alex's taut face.

The shudder of satisfaction she enjoyed was childish, yes, and she shouldn't be playing with fire, but it felt so good to get him back. And the discomfort she would cause him now would go with him long after she popped into her car and disappeared.

Utterly pleased wielding her feminine power, Lauren went to open the door of her car but his hand shot over her shoulder, slamming the door to keep it in place. Before she could catch her breath he had her pinned against the car with that body she'd helped turn to rock. Fire trembled through her, lighting every cell, spreading fast, furiously through her system. Her breasts squashed into the window. The hard plane of his pelvis shoved her hips flush with the car. His knees pressed hers into the door. Reflexively she turned her head toward him, ready to bite his head off, but the heat of his breath against her bare neck stole her words.

"I know exactly what you're doing, Lauren." Like a snake he moved his head around to the other side of her head, and she jerked to avoid him. His lips feathered against her ear. "I've always known."

Her heart raced, felt like it would break the glass of her car door when he pressed more deeply into her. "You're hurting me," she whispered angrily.

He didn't ease up. "No I'm not. You like it. You like the way it feels, I can tell."

Fury mixed with despicable desire. Sweat broke her flesh. Wriggling, she tossed her head back in frustration riding too close on the wave of slick pleasure that was truth.

"Let me go." As strong as she was, she could not beat the pure, raw physical male of him that nature had created to conquer and dominate.

Suddenly she could breathe. He'd stepped back. Air swarmed around her, lifting her skirt, cooling hot skin. She whirled around, ready to slug him.

He lifted both hands in surrender. "I don't care if we play, babe. But if you're going to use your womanly gifts, be ready, because I'll fight back like any hot-blooded man."

He backed to his car. There was no smile of conquest, no teasing spark in the depths of his eyes. The hard lines of his face were as serious as she had ever seen them, serious and determined and infallible.

She didn't breathe until he got in his car. Only after he'd driven out of the parking lot did she pound the top of her car with an angry fist, and blow out air. He'd done it. That feeling from so many years ago was stirring now, coming to life like a slick, devilish cobra, its tongue tickling and teasing, uncoiling inside – just for him.

four

Alex was never careless with a car – even in the reckless years of his youth. And he always drove brand new, expensive automobiles. But that wasn't the reason he drove with caution. Truth was he respected the power behind the machine, had since the accident that had stolen part of his father's brilliant mind, leaving his only son with everything money could buy, with the exception of the unique and wonderful mystery that was a father and son relationship.

It wasn't his way to dwell on past unfortunate events, but he would now – anything to get his mind off Lauren.

He shoved the car into third gear, revving in and around slower-moving cars on the onramp to I -15. He didn't have to get on the freeway, his house was only a few miles away from Center Stage, away from the beguiling woman he'd left in the parking lot just seconds ago. No, he needed the open space, a beckoning stretch of road where he could rev his car into high gear while his body slowly downshifted.

She was something else, he thought, jamming across four lanes and into the fast lane at seventy-five. That little dance she'd done to her car had hooked him, just like she'd wanted, and he'd bit hard and fast. He'd tried to stop himself, but had learned a long time ago that where Lauren was concerned, stopping was a thread next to impossible. She had him easy, and it was too late to dance back.

Whether or not she knew it, she'd had him since junior high school when his adolescent body hadn't known that just being in casual contact with someone could change every hateful cell into yearning.

It had been down hill after that, fast and speedy: like a car out of control he crashed for her. Of course, she thought he despised her, but that attention was better than nothing at all.

It was pathetic; he knew that even then. Everyone thought they had some long-running feud. No one ever saw what was really happening inside of him. His crush had blown out and become a full-fledged obsession.

Feeling his nerves relax a little with memories, Alex down shifted. She was wrong about him. He'd been just as shocked as she when his friends jumped on her like a pack of wolves that night. The sight had filled him with such ferocious anger he knew he'd be capable of killing someone to protect her.

Damian hadn't spoken to him since. Some of the other guys had sloughed out of his circle, but he hadn't cared. All he could think about is what would have happened if he'd not been there.

He'd had plenty of relationships in the four years he was at Princeton, vainly thinking his feelings for Lauren would be lost in the arms of other women. But no one electrified his system the way she did.

He'd been unable to stop keeping tabs on her – even for the sake of curiosity – relentlessly following her dance career, toasting her wins by himself with his most expensive bottle of wine when she placed sixth in Nationals. When she and Peter placed at Blackpool, he'd been in the audience. She hadn't seen him, but he'd been there applauding in standing ovation, along with every other amazed spectator.

It was never easy watching her in the arms of another man, even though he had no right to feel possessive. She'd been married to the man, after all. But Alex felt like she was his, even with that union as real as the fierce heat that smoldered inside of him when he watched them dance.

After her marriage, he resigned himself to being just another one of her admirers. Though months would go by without a sighting of her, he would find himself wondering if she was happy, if her husband loved her. If he worshipped her, owned her, made her feel like he would sacrifice his soul just to keep her at his side.

When Chad told him that they'd divorced, he hurt inside for her, having come to learn how centered she was on their career together. Chad didn't know the details of the divorce, only that it happened soon after their daughter was born.

The news hadn't thrilled him like he thought it might. He believed in the unity of marriage, through joy and sadness, pleasure and pain. It was how he intended to enter into such a commitment.

Alex rubbed his chin and moved over a lane. She was tough. It wouldn't be easy being a single mother. But to be a single mother with a handicapped child, he had to hand it to her for being a fighter. They had that in common; a characteristic Alex knew as well as he knew his inclination to anger.

That was the bottom line of his attraction to her – she was a fighter. She had what it took to stick something out. That she fought him only intensified that attraction.

The road opened. He sped in the lane and thought about how her life was open, his life was open, and he was going to make sure their paths crossed. If she wanted to fight him along the way, he was ready – he'd been ready since junior high, suited up, pumped. Yeah, he was more than ready to take on Lauren.

five

Lauren pulled into the Center Stage parking lot expecting to find it empty. It was after hours, the time when a lot of partnerships practiced without the distraction of the students coming and going.

She saw Chad's white Toyota Tacoma. What she didn't expect to see was Alex's black BMW.

"What is he doing here?" she mumbled, and pulled her car next to his, ready to take her keys and scratch a nice, deep line along the side of it. Unfortunately, her conscience wouldn't allow her the indulgence. She knew why he was there, of course, and suddenly wished she'd worn something other than her baggy grey sweats and scruffy old tee shirt.

She found them in Studio 8, standing in front of the mirror; Chad was teaching Alex the basic step of samba.

Alex wore all black, from snug, body-defining turtleneck sweater to classic silky slacks. The dramatic color didn't swallow him; it electrified him. His black hair stuck up and out as if he'd rammed his hands through it. No doubt from frustration, Lauren smiled wryly. The door closed behind her, announcing her arrival and both men looked over.

The sight of Alex simply sucked the breath out of her chest, leaving her weak in the knees. He scrubbed his head again, then pushed up the sleeves of his sweater.

"Hey, Lauren." Chad crossed to her, oblivious to the sudden tense vibes bouncing off the walls of the room. With his sandy blonde hair, his blue eyes, he looked more like a surfer than a dancer – at least to Lauren.

Whatever Alex was doing there Lauren would not let it affect her performance. Judges, peers and critics, were far more treacherous audiences than annoying playboys.

Dropping her duffle next to the music system, she once again was sorry she had not worn something more form fitting, knowing the power she held over Alex. He'd made her life so unbearable all those years ago, a little intolerable cruelty was the least she could do to finally even the score.

She gave him her pearliest, most artificial smile and extended her hand. "Alex. You're here again." But, hmmm, if he didn't look sleek as James Bond just off some exotic mission.

He shook her hand, then brought it slowly to his lips. Her heart banged. The warmth of his mouth spread across the top of her hand, sending hot rivets up her arm and throughout the rest of her.

"That I am," he said, his hot breath searing her skin. She drew her hand away.

"He told me you're not sure about this, Lauren," Chad said, still unaware of the silent battle going on between them. "I asked him to join us for rehearsal tonight. I think this sponsorship is the best thing. I do."

Alex's brown eyes didn't vary from hers, not even to give Chad a cordial agreement. Lauren smiled deeply. He came to watch her dance? How luscious for him. She turned, ready to cross to the center of the room but caught sight of her grungy outfit and her pleasure at playing with him withered. Of all the nights she could have looked hot. She wanted to kick herself.

"So you're here to watch?" she asked, waiting for Chad to join her so they could begin. "It looked to me like you were here to learn. Wasn't that samba Chad was teaching you?"

Both men crossed to where she stood. "He asked me to

show him, yeah," Chad offered.

"I asked him which dance was the most romantic. He said samba."

"That's his opinion." Lauren lifted her shoulders. "It certainly isn't mine."

Alex blinked slowly, a smile barely creasing his lips. "And what would your opinion be?"

Chad scrambled, "Uh, maybe we should get started."

Alex raised a hand to stop him, his eyes firmly set on Lauren. "No, this interests me. Lauren?"

"Rumba." At once she stepped away from them, breaking into the achingly slow liquid moves, her arms curling, her body beckoning as she looked at him. "Nothing," she lowered her voice, bringing her leg up and around, her toe barely clearing his nose before she held it near her head, then brought it back down in a sweep of elegance. "Nothing is as taunting, as driven by need and passion, as rumba."

She finished her brief display by going back into an impossible arch, swinging her body around so that she came up right in front of his face. His eyes slit briefly; his tongue swept his lips.

Lauren had to smile.

"Of course," she took Chad by the hand, leading him a few feet away, "we'll give you a demonstration. You can decide for yourself."

Alex stood alone with his hands on his hips, his fingers digging. She was hot. Scorching, in fact. He broke into a sweat just watching her in those slow, forbidden moves all by herself. He'd be on fire if he watched her dance with a man. He wanted that man to be him.

The game was on. They were beyond the starting gate.

She'd joined in the fight – willingly – and everything inside of him was challenged now. He wanted her. He'd do whatever it took to have her.

It didn't matter what she wore either. She could make a paper bag look sexy. Those worn sweats told him when it came to getting down and dirty, she wasn't vain about it – it was all about the end result.

He liked that. He was sick of women who wouldn't hit the tennis court unless they were tanned and dressed like Anna Kourninkova. He'd seen enough women who wouldn't go scuba diving or out for a day of boating because it would wreck their mascara to last him a lifetime.

Lauren was beautiful in sweats or beads – she knew it, and she knew everybody else knew it. There was an intrinsic strength in that he liked.

"Let me put on some music," she said suddenly. Alex watched the idle swing of her hips as she crossed the floor. She spent a moment choosing, and Chad jogged over to him, but Alex kept his gaze firmly on her back. He liked her hair up, it reminded him of those saucy ponytails she'd worn in junior high – a time he couldn't forget.

"This is going to work, I know it," Chad whispered. "She'll see the light eventually. I'll make sure of it."

Alex nodded, but his mind was saying, No, *I will make sure of it.*

Drums thudded in a languid beat. Celine Dion's raspy voice sung about seduction, and Alex's blood started the familiar buzz that came with just looking at Lauren.

She crossed to Chad, her hand out, and he took her in his arms. The sight made Alex's neck hot with jealousy.

He couldn't take his eyes off Chad's hands as they

cradled her waist, slipped around her body. Something about it caused the buzz in his blood to skip. She was right, rumba was much more intimate. Their bodies stayed fused. Every move was exact. When they rolled around and around in languid circles, her back pressed into his chest, her head at the crook of his neck, her eyes were closed in sensual submission. Alex almost looked away, the sight so exquisite.

Alex wet his lips. His fingers itched to feel her pressed against him that same way. He wanted to move her – drive her with his own hands, push her with his own body, not stand there and watch.

She was convincing as she touched Chad, her strokes the caress of a luring lover. If he didn't know better, Alex would be completely convinced that the two of them were more than an obligatory partnership.

By the time they finished, Alex's armpits were drenched, his neck coated with sweat, and his heart could not stop its fierce pounding. He applauded and forced himself to appear only slightly impressed.

"I think you're right." He hated giving her even that, knowing how she would gloat. And she did. That smile of hers, the way her lovely brow arched – he knew she was enjoying his concession. "Rumba gets my vote."

He wanted to change the subject and get to what would make her his to do with as he pleased. He rubbed his hands together. "There's no question you two can dance." It surprised him that he felt animosity simmering as he stood close to Chad. He'd never felt competitive with his younger friend, but things were different now that Chad had even a small claim on Lauren.

"I can only see where my financial assistance would

make something good, better."

"What we have is more than good," Lauren corrected him.

Alex was glad she wasn't dismissing the idea of his help. "I'm looking at hiring Rueben La Bate. He's willing to come out of retirement for us. The price is hefty but he's worth it. In addition to carte blanche on all costuming, travel, and competition expenses, I'm willing to give you both a living allowance of three thousand dollars a month."

Lauren couldn't stop her eyes from popping. The instant she saw his face light with pleasure from it; she changed her expression to blank and lifted her chin. Inside, she was humming. Three thousand dollars a month? With the money she made from teaching she'd have six thousand dollars. She'd never seen that much money. Wouldn't either, unless she shook hands with Alex Saunders.

Why did it have to feel as though she was lying on an altar, offering herself, body and soul, to his every whim?

Maybe it was the black intrigue in his eyes, something warning but luring at the same time. Unfortunately, she knew she couldn't common sense her way out of this one – Alex and Chad were unequivocally right. As with most things in life, money made a difference. In competitive ballroom dance, it bought you the best coaches, the most exceptional costuming, and any opportunity a pair chose to compete. It's what she would sacrifice everything for. Was she ready to do that?

"I think we should do it," Chad chirped with the eagerness of a child.

Lauren let out a sigh. The extra money would buy her an ABA program for Rebekah, a one-on-one learning technique proven to actually make a difference in children with autism.

She could finally afford anything and everything she had ever wanted for Rebekah's care and development.

Her heart was tender instantly, and in that moment of vulnerability, she looked at Alex. He was watching her with the intensity of a hawk that had just carried a mouse into the nest to savor later. It would be risky, but she would be the only one to deal with it. Chad wouldn't be hurt by anything Alex could do. He was in agreement with the sponsorship and was oblivious to anything else.

There was too much to gain, even if there was risk, even if working with Alex would challenge her will. No one could take away what was most important to her – her dignity, her pride, and her child. It was her child whose face she saw in her mind as she set her hand in Alex Saunders'.

six

She felt as if she was scored open with a knife, and now Alex could see the most intimate parts of her. It was only a handshake – a verbal agreement. Yet she might as well have reached inside and personally handed him every one of her vital organs. She'd never felt this exposed. For all of the torment he'd caused her back in her youth, she'd been able to go home to people that loved her, to the four walls that had protected her as her battered self-image healed.

Her family was far away now. She had only Rebekah, and the house she lived in suddenly looked like the house of straw the helpless pig tried to hide in. The big bad wolf had made short order of that.

The look on Alex's face was beyond pleased. Something more flickered there – satisfaction so deep it sent a shudder of uncertainty through Lauren. She opened her mouth, hoping to rescind, but he spoke first, his voice calm.

"Then it's final." He reached into his back pocket and Lauren watched him pull out a black wallet, his long fingers stealthily lifting a stack of hundred dollar bills.

Her eyes widened.

"I believe in starting things right," he said. There were two bundles, wrapped in bank tape. He handed one to Chad, who thanked him, and held the other out for Lauren.

Her shocked eyes lifted to his. If she took the money, the deal would be sealed. There would be no going back. She couldn't think selfishly. She couldn't afford to worry about what was coming, if Alex's hatred of her would only deepen because he had some control over her life now. She thought briefly of the desire she witnessed in his eyes – that was fleeting, base. Anyone could have that for the blink that it was. She reminded herself that the alliance would benefit Rebekah first, her and Chad second.

Extending her hand, she didn't look at him when he laid the stack of wrapped bills in her palm.

"This is so awesome," Chad bubbled, stuffing his wad in his back pocket.

"Yes." Alex's voice was smooth and agreeable. Feeling very much like an escort paid for services, Lauren quickly left the two of them and took her money to her bag. Only one thing could bring tears to her eyes, and that was her child. Rebekah's condition was something she had very little control over. She had control over this, she thought, ferociously blinking, angrily sticking the money in her wallet. She didn't have to feel guilty about doing something she needed.

Chad rambled on and on to Alex, but Lauren didn't listen. She forced positive thoughts of Rebekah's possibilities. She would begin looking for a speech therapist, someone who could train Aubrey. Now she would be able to buy Rebekah all of the learning supplies she needed. Turn the extra bedroom into a first rate work room for Rebekah and Aubrey.

Chad called her to the center of the studio and as she approached them, she could barely glance at Alex. The exchange of money had indebted her to him. Sponsorships worked that way; she knew that. It didn't make staring into his satisfied face any easier.

As she and Chad continued to rehearse she told herself she didn't have to give Alex anything she didn't want to. His sponsorship bought him certain rights to them as a pair, to her and Chad as a dancers willing to do their very best to ensure that he get some kind of return on his investment.

She wondered what he could possibly want from this. Yes, he was Chad's friend. But she couldn't help feeling a twist of suspicion at his sudden interest in the sport.

Lauren chanced a look over where Alex sat, watching their every move. With one leg crossed over the other, arms stretched out, he looked too analytical for her liking. He didn't know his right foot from his left, let alone the specific form of cha-cha. If he thought he was going to give them any advice, she'd make it perfectly clear he was not the minute his smug mouth opened.

"That looks good," he said when they finished their cha-cha routine.

"Of course it looks good," she muttered.

Chad leaned over to her. "What's with you?"

They paced opposite each other as they caught their breath. "Nothing."

"He might have heard you."

She shrugged, pulled on the neck of her tee shirt to allow airflow down her sweaty chest. "He's not qualified to say one way or the other."

"Don't blow this before we get a chance," Chad whispered.

Alex unfolded his sleek black form and crossed to them with his hands tucked casually in his front pockets. He wore the smile of an owner whose horse had just won the Kentucky Derby.

"I'll contact Reuben and set everything up."

Lauren lifted her chin at him. "How do you know he'll even accept?"

"He already has." Alex's eyes glittered. His gaze skimmed her face, and she suddenly felt self-conscious. Lifting the hem of her baggy shirt, she wiped herself like a trucker just emerging from a long, hot drive. If Alex thought she cared how she looked in his presence, he was dead wrong. Only after she lifted her shirt did she realize that her abdomen would be bared to him.

It was only a glance, but Alex's gut tightened when he saw the carved lines of her stomach and waist. She was deliberately being casual about this, trying to cover that he'd bought her.

The idea gave him a fast, thick surge of heat. She'd hated shaking his hand, hated that she needed the money. But he'd done his homework and knew that she had enough needs that if she had any common sense at all, she wouldn't turn him down for the sake of a little pride.

It was just the in he was looking for.

He was meeting with resistance. When he'd laid the money in her hand, he thought he saw surrender in her eyes, felt give in her hand. She'd immediately put the funds in her purse, looking half ashamed.

He didn't like that.

During the last few days his desire to get closer to her had only intensified. His appetite couldn't be satisfied with just a sniff – he wanted to taste, savor and swallow her whole.

He didn't mind her being feisty. He enjoyed it. They'd played at being adversaries for so long, to see the real emotion of ignominy in the down cast of her head, in the way she kept her eyes averted, pulled a chord of what was basic and male deep inside of him.

The lady in distress. He knew the type well, had been

duped by enough women using his weakness to get to him more often than he cared to admit. But Lauren's display just moments ago wasn't an act. Women couldn't hide it when they needed help – they only hid it when they had too much pride to ask.

They were a threesome now. How to proceed so she would take his offer seriously and slip off the boxing gloves?

"Yeah," he continued. "Reuben's just waiting for my call."

Lauren's brow arched. "I know Reuben, and he doesn't wait for anybody's call, not anymore anyway."

"He was your coach once." Alex tried patience. "I know you know him. But our conversation was just two days ago. He said he'd do it, and that he would wait to hear whether or not you and I could come to an agreement."

"You told him about us?"

He smiled. "I like that you used the word 'us', but, no. I didn't say anything. Perhaps he's remembering?"

She fanned her face with her hands, shrugged as if she didn't care. "I never mentioned you back then. We only talked about important things."

He bit back the urge to snag her and bring her hot, sweaty body against his. The need to show her she'd better remember that he was important now. He kept his hands safely grounded in his pockets. "Your subject range will be changing then."

She rolled her eyes.

"Uh," Chad broke in, "that'll be great, Alex. We'll work around him. Whenever he wants us, we'll be here."

Lauren crossed her arms and ticked her head Chad's direction. "We all have lives, Chad."

"I'm sure Reuben will be cognizant of that." Alex took the opportunity to reach out a calming hand, but her green eyes shot like lasers where his hand touched her arm.

"Are we done?" She stepped away, more than ready to get out of there. She asked out of habit, something she wouldn't do again. If Alex thought she was going to clear her every move with him, he thought wrong.

"I'd like to speak privately with you, Lauren, if you don't mind," he said.

Something quivered in her chest as she bent over to pick up her bag. He wanted to speak to her privately? She took a deep breath, tried to force the quivering to stop but it didn't.

Chad shook Alex's hand and made a quick exit.

Lauren turned and faced Alex. He walked toward her, head to toe black, intense and dangerously handsome.

"My daughter needs me."

"I won't keep you long."

"If this is about business, there really isn't anything more to discuss. Chad and I will handle everything just like we always have." She lifted her chin a little. "And you can come along for the ride."

His teeth gleamed when he laughed. He was beautiful when he laughed, she thought then. The way he threw his head back, as if completely taken by the act of it. She'd seen him laugh plenty when they'd been kids – when he'd been laughing at her. She'd never seen beauty in it. Now, it horrified her that her heart skimmed her ribs hearing the deep heartiness, enjoying the way his eyes vanished into midnight crescents.

Still, she knew he laughed at her expense and when his dark eyes held hers she stiffened. "I'm more than coming along for the ride, babe," he started, his voice the low rumble of a train just getting its engines fired up. "I own the vehicle."

Her breath came in and out fast. Every fiber and cell seemed to clutch tight. "Let's get this out in the open right now," she said between teeth.

"Yes. Let's."

"You offered to sponsor us. You don't *own* anything. Not me, not Chad. The only thing this sponsorship gives you title to is what Chad and I do when we dance, that's all. Period. If you think for one gigantically huge egocentrically-centered second it's more than that, you just made the worst business decision of your life."

Rocking back on his heels, Alex let out a sigh. "Lauren, Lauren, Lauren." He positioned himself close, so he could smell that anger in her scent, see it flicker gold in her eyes. "I never make mistakes in business. *Ever.* I offered to sponsor you and Chad because I knew exactly what I was doing." He let his gaze drop to her mouth. "I knew exactly what I would get."

If he was getting to her at all, it was hard to tell. She kept that chin of hers indomitably lifted, those eyes as hard as Italian marble. Alex's nerves held.

"What you will get," Lauren spaced the words with great control, "are two competitors who take perfecting their sport seriously. You will get as near perfect performances as humanly possible. *That* is what you will get."

"Good." He inched closer, glad she didn't back away, that their heat mixed and fused, intoxicating him. "But there's one more thing I want from you," he added.

"Forget it," she snapped.

"You haven't heard what it is, yet."

"My imagination tells me—"

"I would love to explore your imagination. Sometime.

For now, I would like you to teach me the samba."

He liked that he startled her with the request. Since she seemed undecided, he slipped his fingers gently under the straps of her bag and eased it from her shoulder. "Please," he said setting the bag quietly on the ground at their feet.

"I really need to get home," she stammered.

He took her hands, held them in his and felt his blood stir just touching her. "Rebekah is with Aubrey until eight-thirty. That gives us forty minutes." Backing toward the center of the room, he kept his eyes on hers, luring her with the gaze.

"How did you know that?"

"I told you, I don't make business decisions unless I know exactly what I'm getting into."

"You…you researched me?"

His lips curved up enticingly. "Of course. I know everything about you." He stopped, slipped his hand around her back, cupped her other hand in his and stood in the only dance position he knew. "I'm sure this is not the correct position to start, but it's the only one I know."

Still digesting that he knew things about her, the wariness on Lauren's face was clear. She stood statue-still in his embrace. "What else do you know about me?"

"Don't get the wrong idea," he said. "This was not some deep, clandestine study. I just checked around. I found out that you've been married, for instance. That you have a child – a child with a handicap. I know your passion for dancing, that you love to teach. I know you're in it for the long haul. That's what I wanted to know before I decided to get involved."

"Oh."

"So, how about it? Will you teach me the rumba?"

"I thought you said you wanted to learn samba?"

"Whatever it was you and Chad were doing earlier. The dance of love, I believe you called it?" She inched back. "That's what you called it, wasn't it?" he asked, noting that she'd pulled away.

"The Latin dances are all dances of love," she said educationally. "They start with cha-cha, the flirtatious dance where a couple teases at love. The lovers progress through samba, and with each dance become progressively more seduced, more deeply... in love."

"Until they rumba?"

"Rumba is the ultimate intimate expression of love, but after that is paso dobles, the matador and the bull."

He grinned. "I like that."

"You would."

"But the union in rumba, that's not the final conquest?"

She shivered, thinking about being conquered – by him. "It can be – it depends on the choreography. *Paso* extends that sexual tension, taking it one step further. A lovers' quarrel maybe—"

"And they make up with great sex afterwards, right?"

She rolled her eyes. "With jive."

"Jive? Sounds like something hip-hop."

"It kind of is, but it's meant to be a very upbeat celebration of love and union."

He pulled her against him. "I'll stick with rumba."

Lauren let out a sigh and tried not to enjoy feeling every part of him nestled against her. She liked the determined male in him, powerful, like a beautiful stallion anxious at the gate.

"Rumba is slow, perfected movements," she explained. "Sometimes partners move together, sometimes they move alone."

"Like life," he observed. "And like love."

"Yes." She took his hand, showing him where to place it high on the center of her back just under her shoulder blade. Then she lifted his other hand out to the side, nestling hers in his fingers.

"The basic is in this position." Easing back, she was amused by the scant disappointment in his eyes when a good foot separated their bodies.

"What was that I saw you and Chad doing, stuff that looked like two soft pretzels twisting around?"

She smiled in spite of herself. "Pretzels? Those were very advanced moves, Alex. As someone very intelligent once said, 'let's start at the very beginning, it's a very good place to start.'"

Demonstrating the basic steps of rumba, Lauren showed him how to shift his weight so it looked like his hips swung seamlessly. Like most men, he found the move more difficult to swallow doing than the physical act itself.

"Men aren't supposed to move like that," he said after an exasperating few minutes.

"You saw Chad? Did he look funny to you?"

"No, he looked great – I can't say that about a guy."

"Get over your phobia." She moved a little closer and set her hands on his hips. "Rotate. Nice and slow now."

When he didn't move, she lifted her eyes to his. They were bright, alive and piercing.

"Your hands," his voice was coarse.

"Are there to help you," she finished his sentence. "Move your hips," she told him. "I will guide you."

He let out a little helpless laugh that shot heat to her cheeks. She kept her face angled at his pelvis. Still, he did not move. She looked up at him again. "Are you going to rotate or not?"

He stepped away, face flushed, and shook his head. "I – I can't do that, not with your hands there. And you're looking at me."

"Because I'm teaching you, hello," she said, trying to stay serious. Wasn't this interesting? "Alex." She spoke in her instructional tone of authority. "I teach little children to do this – and they do it. Are you telling me that a grown man can't swivel his hips?"

"I can swivel just fine, babe," he said, but he kept his distance as if she were reaching out to him with live wires in her hands.

"Okay, then, come over here and swivel."

"It's just – I feel—"

"Get over it. Men dance. Women love men that can dance. Do you have a girlfriend?" He shook his head. Suddenly his eyes changed as they locked with hers.

"A temporary problem I'm sure," she started, trying not to be taken by the intensity on his face. "In any event, women love it when a man can dance with them, so—"

"Do you?"

She tucked a fallen hair behind her ear. "I'm a dancer by profession, of course I like it."

In a few fast steps, he was back in front of her. She looked up at him, her breath quickening. For a flash, she had the strange and outlandish fantasy that he might kiss her right then and there.

She wanted to slap herself for even thinking it. The last thing she would ever do was get involved with her sponsor. Especially if that sponsor was someone she still didn't trust and really didn't know anymore.

He reached for her hands without breaking eye contact, and set them back on his hips. Then he placed his palms lightly on her shoulders. She wanted to say, 'you can do this,' but she'd never be that encouraging to him, even with their alliance. If he wanted to do it, he'd do it without her cheering for him.

His hips began to move in a deliberately slow circle, with her hands riding them. Why it sent a pleasant charge through her, she couldn't say. She'd helped countless men through this exact exercise with the tedium of stirring a bowl of oatmeal.

She dared a look at his pelvis, saw that it was amazingly fluid for a first timer and knew instantly that he had what it took to dance. Hip rotations were the knife of dance, cutting through those that could and could not do the necessary motion with the efficiency of a butcher severing fat from meat.

"Very good," she told him. Let him think I'm only mildly impressed, she thought, though her amazement grew as his slow circles became even more liquid.

She stood back, and he stopped.

"Why did you stop?" she asked.

"I'm not going to dance here like a hula dancer."

His self-depreciating sense of humor appealed to her, if not surprised her for a man who had everything. She assumed his cockiness wouldn't have room for anything less than permanent back patting, even in the name of humor.

"Are you ready for more or was that enough for one day?" she asked.

He closed the space between them and pulled her in his arms again, too close for rumba, but the smile on his face told her he didn't care. "Bring it on, babe."

seven

With three thousand extra in the bank, Lauren went to work searching for the intensive applied behavioral application program she always dreamed of for Rebekah but wasn't able to afford.

Researchers agreed aggressive intervention often produced the best results. One of the best ways to teach was in small classroom settings, with a teacher working one-on-one with the child.

Lauren found a small group of developmental practitioners specializing in autism spectrum disorders called Giant Steps. She liked it because it was close to home. An old, turn-of-the-century church house had been donated, renovated and turned into a place where children ages three to five could be placed with highly trained teachers for the daily eight-hour long sessions.

She was set to rehearse with Chad, but Lauren decided to stop by the dilapidated-looking building surrounded by a chain-link fence just to see if there were any openings in the program. A small, rickety play set sat in a sand yard and a handful of children and adults were there. The children didn't swing, climb or do anything else like normal children do with a play set. Lauren was not surprised. One little girl stood trailing her finger up and down one of the poles. Rather than swing, another little girl simply twisted the seat, watched it untwist, only to repeat the action over and over. A boy plopped in the sand, picked up handfuls, and slowly let the sand drain from his fingers. None of the children talked.

Inside, the halls echoed with the screams and howls known well by parents whose children suffered with the ailment. Sometimes those were the only sounds the children ever made. A musty scent of old wood tickled her nose.

Lauren was greeted in the large, empty foyer of the building by a smiling Tiffany Tucker, a petite woman in her early thirties. She wore her golden raisin-colored hair back, baring ivory skin with a smattering of freckles across her nose.

"We have a very intensive program here at Giant Steps," Tiffany began, leading Lauren on a tour. They stopped in the old chapel, now gutted to be a multi-purpose room where mats covered the floor and therapists took the children through some exercises.

"Our staff is all special ed trained with an extra two years in autism education as well, so they're uniquely qualified to handle the needs and interests of children with autism."

They moved to a classroom where eight teachers sat scattered around the room, a child placed in a chair directly in front of them for one-on-one teaching. Lauren watched with interest as the teachers spoke animatedly, sometimes loudly, sometimes softly, to the children in an effort to get and keep their attention.

"In this room they teach basic attending skills," Tiffany continued, "so that the children can move on to academic and social skills in the other classrooms. Has Rebekah had any attending work done?"

Lauren nodded. "I've had a girl working with her for a year now. She's coming along, but slowly." She couldn't wait for Rebekah to be a part of something wonderful like this.

Tiffany nodded, leading her down the hall. "Slow is normal for autism. But the end goal is functionality. We do everything in our power for the eight hours they are here to see to it that we pack in as much behavioral work as we can. Some of our graduates are mainstreamed by the time they are five. Some go on to attend regular school with just a little help. But those are extreme cases. I have to be honest with you, most of the children are still classified with autism even after the heavy early intervention."

"I'm not looking for a miracle cure." Lauren knew no such thing existed. Progress would be miracle enough. "As long as she continues to go in the right direction, I'm happy."

They passed a small library with computers, a few shelves of books and an old TV. As Tiffany explained the program, what they could offer Rebekah as well as Lauren in the way of support, Lauren's enthusiasm grew.

Tiffany smiled as they came to a double door. The scent of food snuck out. "Our cafeteria is in here." Tiffany opened the doors.

"Rebekah's on the Gluten Free, Casein Free diet," Lauren informed her.

Tiffany nodded. "As are many of our students. We serve both here. Some of the parents send their own food, in an effort to cut down the cost."

Two adults sat at one of three long tables where a handful of children were spread out, eating. A little girl was standing on one of the tables flapping her hands and the teacher patiently set her back in her seat.

"There is a year-long waiting list," Tiffany said. "I didn't know if my secretary told you."

Lauren's heart sank. "No, she didn't."

"She hates to disappoint parents. I'm sorry. I hope this wasn't a waste of time for you."

"Not at all." But Lauren was devastated. Every day they waited meant stagnancy in Rebekah's growth and development.

They walked back to the office where Tiffany handed Lauren a file so she could fill out some paperwork. "Let's get you started, and then you'll be on the list," she said.

Lauren sat, filling out the pile of paperwork with a heavy heart. She wanted this more than anything. For all that money she now had, she still could not get Rebekah what she needed most. There might as well have been a rope tied around her wrists.

After she'd filled out the file, she shook Tiffany's hand. Money, she thought grimly as she walked to her car, was not the key to everything.

*   *   *

She'd tied herself to Alex and for what? Driving to the studio, Lauren's frustration grew. Pounding the steering wheel, she shouted at a driver pulling a right turn from the middle of the lane. "Idiot!"

Up until now, she hadn't put Rebekah's name on any waiting lists because she hadn't known when she would be able to afford it, should Rebekah be admitted. The money – Alex Saunders' money – now sat in her bank without real purpose.

Of course she wanted the perks of sponsorship, but that's all they really were – first class perks. Her life wouldn't change any. She would continue to teach, continue to practice with Chad, chasing the championships they both wanted. But her child – that was why she shook Alex's hand.

To find his car at the studio heated her frustration. She stormed in, ready to bite somebody's head off.

Today, Alex wore dark brown, and looked like imported chocolate, delectable and deadly. Her body went into an **automatic fizz when their eyes met. That irritated her even** more.

Chad was showing him more of rumba, and as she crossed the floor, she could see they'd moved on to advanced steps. Who did he think he was? Two lessons and he was already doing advanced? Beyond reasonable now, Lauren dropped her bag, changed her shoes into the arched nightmare shoes worn for ballroom, eyeing the shoes resentfully as she approached.

"You're doing great." Chad bubbled with enthusiasm she would never give Alex. "You're a total natural. Don't you think, Lauren?"

It didn't take much to light her brittle wick. "He's doing all right I suppose. I thought Reuben was coming?"

She could see Alex had read her nasty mood. "He's on his way."

Lauren let out a little hiss of annoyance. "He never used to be late."

"Guess he's rusty," Alex said.

"You want to try the steps with Lauren?" Chad suggested.

"I'd like that very much." But Alex didn't move, too aware of Lauren's disposition.

"I bet you would," Lauren muttered.

"Everything okay?" Alex asked.

"Fine," she snapped. She could apologize to Chad, innocent as he was, caught in the web of her tangled disappointments, but Alex was the very thread woven in the web.

When the door opened, her heart lifted at the familiar face of her old coach. She'd adored Reuben all those years ago, had sweated for him, endured blisters for him, cried for him, and won titles under his strict ethic of perfection. Now she taught her students the same way.

She skipped over, throwing herself around him. They spun in a joyful hug.

"Look at this," Reuben muttered cheek pressed to cheek. "Look at what I found." He eased her down, holding her face between his palms. "Who's this beautiful lady, huh? How long has it been? Six years?"

"Too long," she laughed, eyeing the smooth dark chocolate of his skin. "And you still look twenty-nine. You're amazing."

"Last time I saw you was at a comp, about six years ago I think. You were dancing with Peter, right?" She nodded, awestruck just like she used to be in his presence. "And now you're at it again?"

"I'm at it again. Have you met Chad?" She hooked her arm in his and led him to where Alex stood with Chad.

"Seen the boy dance, but never met him." Reuben stuck out his hand. "Pleased."

"Honored." Chad's eyes were huge. "And this is Alex."

"We've met." Alex gave Reuben a cordial nod.

"So, you came out of retirement." Lauren looked up at him.

"I was getting itchy feet. I kept telling Gail it was time I found some kids to whip into shape."

"And here we are. Be ruthless, brutal," she told him. "Chad and I want to leap up the charts this year."

"Have I ever been anything but?" Reuben patted her

arm then clapped his hands, his long-time signal that it was time to get started. "Let's see what you two can do. Start from the top of your standard routine."

Chad put on some music, and Lauren waited alone in the center of the room. There was only one chair and Alex offered it to Reuben who shook his head, firmly crossing his arms, resting his chin in his fingers, ready to study.

Alex placed the chair next to the wall and sat.

Crying violins slowly filled the air. For a brief second, the weepy strains reminded Lauren of her predicament with Rebekah. Music could hit her like that, fast and sharp in the heart. Sad melodies were the worst. Like darts they flew past her defenses and struck her soul.

She was glad to be there, even with Alex observing – a dark image out the corner of her eye. She shifted her thoughts to dance, to that place alone where her feet would carry her and offer a reprieve from her worries.

Reuben walked a slow circle around them his green eyes flicking from their footwork to their hand work to body motions. It had been years since he'd coached her, but Lauren remembered well his many looks. He rubbed his naked head when he was frustrated, lifted his brow when annoyed, and pressed his fingers together when he was uncomfortable with something. Those green eyes of his could cut through any imperfection, and you couldn't fake it. If you missed a step, your toe wasn't where it was supposed to be, he caught it, and you heard about it.

When Lauren and Chad had gone through the entire ten dances, they paced, catching their breath while Reuben stood still in thought. Chad glanced at Lauren nervously, but she winked at him. They'd done well. She felt it in their bodies, completely unified throughout the dances. Not that she cared about making mistakes – Reuben was there to fine tune and if he saw flaws, she wanted to know about them.

"Looks damned good," he finally said. "I'm impressed. Chad, you the man." He patted Chad's shoulder with a smile. "Technique is strong. The only place I can see improvement is in the choreography. It could be notched up a little. Sassier. Sexier." He waited for Lauren and Chad to agree. They exchanged looks, finally nodding at each other, their breath slowing to an even pace.

"Great. Then let's start at the beginning."

The remaining two hours were spent changing their Latin routines. Reuben was known for innovative choreography, implementing moves that balanced on the razor's edge of what conservative judges found acceptable yet pushed right to the boundary line.

"I want more heat. You're both going through the motions, and I see plenty of expression on your faces, but I want to feel the sizzle when you come together. You're not a couple are you? Privately?"

Both Chad and Lauren shook their heads. Lauren noticed Alex shifting in his seat after Reuben posed the question. "Do either of you have a significant other?"

Again, they both shook their heads. Lauren glanced over at Alex: why, she wasn't sure, but when his gaze locked on hers her heart fluttered uncontrollably. If he thought she was even considering the idea of him, she'd show him how ineffective those hot looks were on her.

"Actually," she said suddenly, "I do have someone."

Chad's head tilted toward her but Reuben only smiled. "I should have figured as much. You're too gorgeous not to have them lined up. Anyway, you both could use with a little visualization. I know you're buddies, and sometimes the casual nature of partnerships can leak in. We want to seal that leak, keep the audience wondering if you're more than partners. Create heat."

"Try it again, and think about that special someone."

As Chad took her in his arms in the basic of cha-cha, he leaned near her. "What if I don't have anybody?"

"Think Sports Illustrated Bathing Suit Issue."

Chad grinned. "Gnarly."

eight

It took the mere thought of one of the sexy women for Chad to give that extra punch to his performance. Reuben complimented him, told him that whatever he'd done, to bring it to the floor every time he danced.

Lauren didn't think of anyone, just dreamed. Sometimes that was enough, thinking about winning, about taking the title. She rarely thought of a man when she wanted to coat her moves with sensuality. After dancing with Peter, Lauren considered dance separate, an act done in unity but still utterly solo.

Reuben didn't say much about her performance, and she wondered why. As he bid Chad good-bye for the night, she began to fret. Once the studio door closed and Chad was gone, Alex joined Reuben and the two engaged in a quiet head-to-head chat.

Lauren didn't like that at all and promptly crossed the floor to them.

"So," she interrupted without any concern whatsoever. "What'd you think, Reuben?"

They both turned to her. Reuben's eyes held that sharp blade of uncertainty she had seen in her youth just before he'd cut the toes off one of her confident performances.

"Not bad, sis," he started.

Alex stayed with them in their huddle and her brows lifted, as if to say, *get lost*. But he didn't move.

"It's been a while," Reuben went on, "and I have to admit, I haven't been following what's up with you. But whatever it is, I can see it."

Lauren's skin heated. Her chin lifted in response. She was sure what deeply troubled her could never be seen through a perfect performance. "What do you mean?"

"I mean something's buggin' you. And it's not just that you didn't sleep well last night or there's a bunion on your toe. It's part of you."

She faced him straight on, ignoring Alex's face in her side vision. "You've never seen it before."

Reuben lifted a shoulder. "It wasn't there before. Don't freak out about it." He set his hands on her shoulders. She fought shirking away; she could hardly stand the chastisement with Alex standing right there.

"Is there something I can do?" Alex interjected. Lauren read the sincerity in his eyes but wouldn't take it. She knew Reuben gave advice. But he rarely involved himself in his students' personal lives. He expected them to fix their own problems.

"No." Her tone was icy for a reason. "This doesn't involve you."

The concern in his brown eyes hardened suddenly. "If it involves you, it involves me."

"Like hell it does," she shot back, facing him now. Reuben took a step back from both Lauren and Alex. "I told you, I don't owe you anything but the best I have."

"Apparently that wasn't your best today."

"And how would you know? You don't know anything about dance."

"You heard it from the expert here." Alex gestured to Reuben before ramming his hands into his hair, letting out a growl. "You can be so…so…"

"Stubborn," Reuben finished for him with a nod. "She always has been fire on a spit."

"Excuse me?" Lauren stepped back, incensed.

Both Reuben and Alex smiled, and that made it even worse. She stormed away in a tight pace, mumbling.

"It won't make a difference, if you deal with it." Reuben went to her. His assuring tone slowed her jagged movements, and she looked at him.

"It's bigger than that," she said, almost a weary whisper.

"I'm sorry." Reuben's brows cinched tight. "But if you're going to do this, you have to deal with *that* – whatever *that* is."

He left then, after they set up another time for rehearsal and after he kissed her cheek with a wish for good luck. She pressed her forehead to the door. The disappointment she thought she could dance around draped her shoulders with the weight of a heavy blanket.

She closed her eyes, felt the cold steel of the door chill her to the bone. Timing was everything, and she'd missed an opportunity for Rebekah because money and timing had not come together. She'd have to wait. Lost in disillusionment, she barely felt Alex's presence behind her but when she took in a deep breath, his scent snuck into her senses, and she opened her eyes.

"You sure you're all right?" His voice was soft, sincere. It swept into her chest, welling in a surge of emotion from a barren place she'd learned to refuse notice. Living alone, she allowed much of what caused her vulnerability to wither, afraid of being hurt, ashamed of showing that it mattered.

Tears fought their way into her eyes, but she closed them, making sure they were dry before she turned and faced

Alex. "I'm fine," she said.

His dark eyes studied every inch of her face, trying to understand.

"I should go." She made a move to go around him but his arm shot out, palm against the door to block her.

"Not yet," he said. "We have some things to talk about."

Deliberately she took a slow, scathing scan starting at his feet, working her way up to his eyes. "What could we possibly have to talk about now?"

Alex knew if eyes were flames he would have been scorched by the glare she gave him. He shuddered dramatically, so she saw that he had enjoyed every moment of her scouring gaze. Then he placed his other hand on the door, and caged her in with a grin.

"What you're wearing, and I'm not talking about this, though fetching as it is. Costumes."

Her eyes went hard. "Forget it."

"I won't forget it because I want a say in what you wear."

"Absolutely not."

"If I'm paying for beads, sequins, diamonds and all that jazz, you can bet that soft, sweet mouth of yours I'm going to see every yard of fabric that touches your body if I have to drape you in it myself."

Lauren's eyes shot wide. Inside, she was trembling. She rationalized it could be the cold metal door pressing into her back but she knew better. He said her mouth was soft and sweet. And the very idea of him draping fabric around her knocked her knees into butter.

"I can do this with Chad, if you don't think you can handle it," he said. "Then he and I can make all of the decisions."

"Oh, yeah, right." Her knees still wobbled. His breath tickled her face. She could smell the musk of sweat on his skin. "He'd love it if you cornered him with his back against the wall like this."

A slow grin lifted his lips. "Wouldn't be as much fun. But he'd be a lot more agreeable than you, I can guarantee that."

"I thought you never backed away from a challenge."

"I don't." He stood back, uncaging her. "But with you, anything's possible. Now, I had some drawings done up. Beads, diamonds, rhinestones, fringe, ruffles – everything. The guy's a designer in Hollywood. Will you at least look at them?"

She liked that he asked her, not told her. And it did sound spectacular. Anyone he knew would be top shelf, four star. "Of course. I can be reasonable, you know."

He laughed, and she stole the moment to admire it. When the laugh filtered away, the dark seriousness in his eyes reached out to her bruised hopes. He lifted his hand to her face, his fingers lightly skimming her cheek. "If there's anything you need at all," his voice was that calm, gentle tone of someone who could shoulder everything, "Let me know, Lauren. I mean it."

It would be so easy to unload, to open her heart and allow him a look. But he could hurt her even more if he knew how deeply she felt about loss, love and impossibilities. A man living in a glass house of perfection would never understand how breakable it was in the world outside.

"I can deal with my own problems," she said, stepping past him, breaking the moment.

"I know you can. You're one of the toughest women I've ever known."

She bent over and picked up her bag. "Yeah, well, I've had to be." She slung the strap over her shoulder as he approached. He looked down into her eyes.

"Let me take you to dinner this Friday night. We can look over the designs. Talk."

Her dates were scant and far between because few men wanted to have anything to do with her once they found out she had a child with autism – too much baggage. But she wasn't about to go out on some pity date with her business partner.

"Thanks, but, no."

"Why not?"

"I have other plans." She started toward the door, heard him quickly catch her pace. She looked over at him, saw that his jaw turned to stone.

"Plans? You don't really have someone you're seeing, do you?"

"Of course." She flung open the door. "Don't you believe me?"

She barely had time to take a breath, his hand snapped around her bicep hard as a metal cuff. His eyes bore into hers, flickering with fury. "Who is he?"

At first she just stared at him, then her eyes darted to where his fingers whitened her flesh. "Let go of me."

"*Who is he?*"

"None of your business." Yanking free, she didn't say another word.

Alex watched her walk to her car and shoved his hands into his front pockets, needing to tear into something. He blew out air.

"That's where you're wrong, babe," he murmured. "You

are my business." She backed out her car without looking at him again and jealousy scratched in his veins. Pulling out his cell phone, he dialed.

nine

Who did he think he was? Lauren stepped on the gas pedal, shooting a glance at where his fingers were still imprinted on her bare arm. The nerve, handling me like some fluff girlfriend in a high school drama.

Alex had a long way to go when it came to dealing with women.

Still, a shudder of satisfaction had shot through her when he'd looked at her as if she was breaking some unspoken vow between them. That shudder was still vibrating deep inside, like a harp, freshly plucked, sending delicious chords to every cell.

It was bothersome that she enjoyed their bickering. It went against everything she had ever been taught about peace, love, and harmony. Certainly her parents fought with spice and cream, and they managed to stay together all these years.

Maybe she should take him up on his dinner offer, if for no other reason than to see how easy it was to manipulate him. There would be the added benefit of an evening away from the stress of Rebekah. A free dinner…

You sound desperate and despicable, she told herself, pulling onto her street. While she wasn't at all adverse to doing whatever she had to for Rebekah, she'd never stoop to using someone for her own self-gratification, something she was certain Alex did with the ease of tying one of his designer ties.

She pulled into the driveway with a sigh. Home was not a restful place at this juncture in her life. Rebekah was difficult to handle, a larger than life baby with unspoken needs Lauren was often forced to decode without an interpreter.

Her life and the grey quagmire it was sunk in when she walked to the front door, feeling the weight ready and waiting for her outstretched hands.

The floor was covered with objects, as if Rebekah had taken every drawer and emptied it, running through each room and hall. Lauren forced herself to count to twenty.

Having heard the door open, Aubrey came around the corner with Rebekah squirming on her hip. "Sorry, we were just trying to clean up."

Lauren took Rebekah from Aubrey and gave her an unwelcome squeeze. "Hey, looks like you've been busy." Squealing, grunting, Rebekah shimmied out of her arms, disappearing down the hall.

With a sigh, Lauren sat on the floor with Aubrey and together they gathered the scattered items. "Sometimes I think I should just live with furniture and nothing else," Lauren said wearily.

"How was practice?" Aubrey asked.

Lauren picked up the egg slicer Rebekah loved to pluck. "Fine."

"You like your new dance partner, don't you?"

"He's a great dancer, yes. I was lucky to have found him." Aubrey let out a little sigh and Lauren looked at her. "Anything happen with that guy you were telling me about?"

"That's over."

"Already?"

"He was a jerk."

"Uh-um. Want to tell me about it?"

"He's not worth talking about. I'm thinking of forgetting about guys for a while."

"That can be liberating." Lauren forced a laugh. "Look what it's done for me." They both laughed then. Lauren's mood lifted when her heart opened and she gave advice. "You're still young yet, Aub. You'll meet lots of guys. And you're too sweet to waste time with anyone who doesn't see all of your special qualities."

Aubrey's cheeks pinked innocently. "You're nice."

"I'm right. Seriously, men can be such pains in the—" The ringing phone cut her off and Lauren jumped up and answered it. "Hello?"

"I'm trying again."

The deep, coarse voice shot heat through her system, instantly melting her insides. Why she was smiling like a schoolgirl, she couldn't fathom. "Is that so?"

"I don't give up easily," Alex said.

"I had a bulldog like that once," Lauren teased. She looked at Aubrey and rolled her eyes, pointing at the receiver tucked next to her ear.

Aubrey started putting the piles they had accumulated away with an inquisitive smile on her face.

"Was he your best friend?" Alex asked.

"He was better than that. He rolled over at my command, did whatever I wanted, whenever I wanted."

Alex made a little sound of pleasure in the phone. "Well I'm willing to ask you to dinner again. It's not quite rolling over, but I'd be willing to let you scratch my belly afterwards if you felt so inclined."

She laughed. "You can't be that desperate, Alex. Where are all the women in your life? Come on, I know you."

"I really am not a player."

"And the Pope wears a bathing suit."

"I'm serious. I'm monogamous."

"You mean when you finally settle on just one?" Lauren felt a tingling sensation she hadn't felt in years. She glanced around for Aubrey who had finished the clean up and was mouthing that she was going to go check on Rebekah. Lauren nodded.

"I'm on a mission now," he said.

"Oh? What's that?"

"To show you those drawings. They look great and I can't wait until Friday for you to see them."

"But we didn't have a date for Friday, remember? I told you—"

"I know what you told me." She heard his voice go tight. She couldn't say why that pleased her, but it did. "You said you had other plans. That's why I'm calling you now."

"I can wait until next week to look at the designs, Alex."

"Yeah? Well maybe you can, but I want you to see them. Then we can make a decision, and I can give the designer the go-ahead."

"Gee, I'd like to be able to accommodate you, but I really don't see any place I can fit you in."

"Is that right?" he finally said. "Well, maybe your boyfriend can wait an hour or two while we go over the designs. After all, comp's coming up. But then maybe you'd rather wear one of your older dresses. The judges will appreciate that they don't have to think about considering your costuming because they've already seen it."

She squeezed the phone in her hand. "Any of my has-been dresses would compete quite nicely at any comp, I'll have you know."

"Hey, no argument there, I've seen the dresses and they

are – well, they're nice enough."

"Now you're trying to be annoying."

"I'm trying to get you to come up for air long enough for me to show you what I have in mind so my people can get started. Think you can manage that, Lauren?"

He was really riled. This boyfriend thing was eating at him like a rat at a scrap of cheese. That she held the cheese, made him crawl to it, only sweetened the moment.

"You're asking a lot," she started, a smile still on her face. "We spend every moment we can together, and I don't think he's going to like giving even a second of that up."

There was a long silence, and Lauren set her thumbnail between her smiling lips.

His voice was taut as a drum. "Is that right?"

"Mm-hmm. He's very possessive." Her limbs covered with goose bumps as she squelched a laugh. "Tell you what, I'll talk it over with him – see what I can do."

"Yeah, you do that."

"But Alex," she started, innocence lining her tone, "you sound angry. Is there a problem?"

"The problem is that I'm serious about this and you don't seem to be."

"Of course I'm serious about it." It amazed her how much she enjoyed their conversation. "I want to see the dresses, but first things first."

He cleared his throat into the phone, an obvious message that he didn't approve of her priorities.

Aubrey's face was white when she darted into the room. "Rebekah's gone!"

"What?"

"I went in to check on her and the window – she'd

opened it. She must have crawled out."

Dropping the phone, Lauren ran back to Rebekah's bedroom. Sure enough the sliding window was open just far enough to allow Rebekah's small form to fit through. She ran to the window, pushed it open and searched the backyard. Rebekah was nowhere in sight.

Lauren's heart pounded. The reality of what had happened set in, thick with dread.

"Go next door," she told Aubrey. "Both sets of neighbors know about Rebekah. See if they'll help us look for her."

Aubrey nodded and vanished.

In the silence of her small house, Lauren fought the first clutch of fear. Rebekah was prone to run, like a lot of children with autism. Inexplicably, like a feather in the wind, she would take off. But Lauren or Aubrey had always been at her side, able to stop her. How many times had they chased after her? How many times she had scolded her, uselessly scolded, and begged her not to do it again?

Lauren didn't even know Rebekah could open her bedroom window.

Her knees felt loose, like she might buckle over if she didn't sit, but there was no time for that.

Please, God, wherever she is, take care of her, she prayed, racing out the door.

She stood in the back yard, shouting for her, but knew it was futile. Rebekah never answered to her name, not even with indiscernible babblings. She simply did not understand that when her name was called, she was supposed to reply.

Like a lot of newer houses, the small area wasn't fenced. Owners struggled just to put yards in, let alone costly fences. Which meant Rebekah could be anywhere.

Lauren rounded the house, heading to the front yard.

Already a handful of neighbors had gathered. Missy next door carried a baby on her hip, but she offered to strap him in his car seat and drive around, searching. Jim and Felicity, who lived on the other side of the street, volunteered to split up and search. Mrs. Patterson, an elderly widow across the street, looked forlorn and had tears in her eyes.

"It's okay." Lauren put her arm around the woman's bony shoulders, glad someone could cry. It was something she wanted to do but wouldn't allow.

"She's such a sweet little angel," Mrs. Patterson muttered.

"Yes, she is." Lauren felt her own tears gather and blinked hard. "We'll find her, we will. Aubrey, call the police department, see if we can get somebody out here."

"I'll wait here for you," Mrs. Patterson blew her nose, "so that you can go look."

"That would be great." Lauren gave her another hug.

Just as Aubrey took the steps up into the house, two black and white vehicles came down the street. They pulled up in front, followed by Alex's black BMW. He was out of his car in a flash, his eyes locking with Lauren's as he shook hands with the officers. Alex all jogged over, followed by the police officers.

"Alex." Lauren was surprised that just the sight of him helped ease the burden dropped suddenly on her back. "How did you know?"

"I could hear you over the phone." He reached out and took her hand. "What happened?"

"The window – she opened it and crawled out."

"How long has she been gone?"

"About ten minutes." Lauren rubbed her hands at her

face. "She could be anywhere. Do you know how fast she runs? She's so fast. She's like a runaway puppy. She sees an open space and…and she just goes."

Alex nodded, the line between his brows deepening with concern.

"I'm going to get in my car and go down toward the canal," Aubrey said.

Lauren's heart stopped then, thinking about the snaking canal filled with streaming water just blocks away. Rebekah loved water. Unconsciously she clutched at Alex's arms.

"The canal. She loves the water!"

"You stay here." Alex rubbed her arms soothingly and looked at the officers. "I'll go check it out."

"Can I get a description from you, ma'am?" One of the officers stepped forward. His stomach poured over his taut belt. He waited behind reflective sunglasses.

Lauren nodded, numb. Pressing her hand to her forehead, she watched Alex run with the other officer and get into the police car.

Aubrey stood close. "Want me to stay here instead?"

Lauren slipped her arm in Aubrey's, scraping inside for strength, fighting back tears. Her mind flashed merciless images of her child's innocent, content face, of Rebekah's naive curiosity drawing her to the dangerous edge of the water, where she might reach out to touch, then fall helplessly in.

"How old is the child, ma'am?"

"What? Oh, five."

"What was she wearing?"

Lauren's mind could only see flailing arms and tiny legs lost in rushing water. Her stomach rolled and pitched, her knees gave and the next thing she knew she was sitting on the grass in a daze with the officer crouched on one side, Aubrey on the other.

"You all right, ma'am?"

No, I'm not all right, she wanted to scream. My little girl is running and she has no idea where she is going or how dangerous it is. She doesn't know about cars, she won't look before crossing the street. She's just running.

"What's she wearing, Aub?" Lauren asked, unable to conjure Rebekah's image that day.

As Aubrey described Rebekah's outfit, Lauren stood, feeling itchy to do something. Night was creeping into the sky, and soon the forbidding darkness would prevent them from seeing anything.

"I should go—" She started on a run, where, she didn't know, but she knew she would not be able to stop until Rebekah was found.

"Ma'am!" Fast on her heels was the heavy-set police officer. Lightly he touched her elbow, but she didn't stop. "Ma'am, it'd be best if you stayed here."

"It would be best if I looked, officer." She gathered speed and so did he, his keys and cuffs jangling.

"At least let me take you in the car," he panted.

"A car can't sneak in and out of things like a child can," she shot over her shoulder. Soon, he sloughed off and she didn't hear him anymore.

Where should she start, she wondered, realizing she was heading in the wrong direction. She doubled back, ignoring the small crowd now gathered in her front yard. The officer was still bent over trying to catch his breath.

Lauren headed to the back of her house, then took off through her neighbors' yards, trying to trace where Rebekah might have gone. When she came face to face with a fence, she rounded it, staying on the sidewalk.

It was times like this her soul felt as if she'd been pressed through a shredder. Autism seemed to be the merciless teeth tearing through her, leaving her painfully aware of just how fragile and useless she was in its mighty, obdurate jaws. Her child was not hers, not even in the very normal sense of the word parenting. It seemed she fought a beast inside of Rebekah for ownership.

It was easy to hate that beast when it took over like it did today, changing her child into something driven, obsessed, every other care abandoned for the sake of chasing the fixation.

Scattered in her mind were thoughts of Rebekah. How she could sit for hours with a tiny car in her fingers, driving it along every baseboard in the house. She was also prone to turning on the water faucet and just feeling the water run through her fingers. Knowing nothing of consequence, Rebekah barely noticed when the sink overflowed and water cascaded down the cabinets, onto the floor.

As the street ended and became a T, Lauren's heart sunk. Which way should she go? Which way could have lured her child? It was a toss up, as both ends had equally as many houses and yards.

And straight ahead sat a white house with green shutters.

Out of nowhere, a police car came barreling toward her. She could see through the front windshield that Alex was in the car. They pulled up in front of the house with green shutters and Alex threw open the door, waving her over.

Lauren's heart flew up to her throat and pounded, and she bolted across the street, joining Alex and the officer as they approached the front door.

Alex took her elbow. "They just got a call. She's here."

"What?"

The officer knocked on the door. "A lady called saying a little girl just opened her front door and ran in."

Lauren tried to catch her breath but the run had sucked every ounce of adrenalin and energy from her muscles, and she suddenly felt weak. She looked up into Alex's face. There was concern there, and willingness to share the fear, the aching trapped inside. His arms, strong and supportive, wrapped around her, and she pressed into him, her eyes closed. "Thank God," she murmured.

ten

Lauren stood in Rebekah's bedroom door. The peaceful sight of her child asleep, tucked safely in her bed filled her chest with emotion. Blinking back the rush of tears, she wondered how many more times her heart would have to endure such a savage experience.

Unable to pull herself away from the comforting sight even for a minute, Lauren let out a sigh, and wiped her eyes. How much she looks like a normal child lying there adrift.

It was a blessing that Rebekah had run into the woman's house. Beverly Pendergast had been scrapbooking at her kitchen table when the front door had flung open and a little girl had burst in.

"She just ran right in and started looking around, talking to herself," Beverly told Lauren, Alex, and the officer. "When she wouldn't look at me, or answer me, I knew something was wrong." That was when Beverly called the police.

"I looked outside, thinking she'd just run in from a walk along the street with her mommy perhaps. But there was no one there. Funny thing is I always keep my door locked. I guess I must have forgotten after I got home from the grocery store."

Thank heavens for that, Lauren thought now, still soaking up as much of Rebekah's quiet form as she could.

Even hours later, her heart was swollen; thudding with the possibilities of what could have happened. She would never let Rebekah out of her sight again. But even thinking that caused her body to ache under the pressure of it. There was no way she could change her life to fulfill that decision, the ramifications too extensive. She closed her eyes and willed the never-ending thoughts to leave her. Still, she could not put a price on her child's safety, even for the sake of her own wants.

Overwhelmed, weary, she silently backed out of Rebekah's bedroom, sensing a presence behind her. She forgot that Alex had been there through it all. He didn't say anything when he came up behind her, just set his hands on her shoulders in that familiar, comforting way a husband would to his wife.

The urge to rest her head against him was overwhelming. Nothing would bring her more solidarity, but she hardly knew him and would not touch him in any way that might lead him to think she had inappropriate feelings.

It had been such a blur after they'd found Rebekah. She hadn't had a moment to thank any of her neighbors, all of whom had come over to express their gratitude that her baby was found.

Aubrey, dear sweet Aubrey, had shadowed Lauren like a little sister. With all the commotion, she'd offered to bathe Rebekah and get her ready for bed. But Lauren needed to do that perfunctory job herself, so she excused Aubrey for the rest of the night.

With Alex's hands firmly on her shoulders, she shut her eyes, so ready to fall into sleep that when he turned her around, she hardly noticed, until she opened her eyes and found herself looking into his calming face.

"Big day," he said.

She nodded. How she wanted to be held just then, told everything was going to be okay, that she could do whatever was necessary for her child and she'd still make it through. It had been so long since a man had held her with the exception of dance; her body craved that cradled feeling of total comfort.

Because no one could offer her what she craved, she felt a sudden flash of frustration and disappointment. She stepped back, and passed him, leaving him in the darkened hall. The house was still tidy after she and Aubrey picked up, so she stood in front of the window, looking out into darkness.

In the reflection, she saw Alex follow her, but he kept his distance.

"I can't imagine how you must be feeling now," he said, his tone reticent. "Has this happened a lot?"

She shook her head but didn't turn to face him; instead she watched him in the reflection of the glass. "Not like this. When it has, Aubrey or I have been with her and we've chased after her."

"And no one knows why she runs?"

Again, she shook her head. "But it's common among children with autism."

"Interesting," he murmured. He was slowly moving closer. Not in a seductive way, just in the way one human in need would approach another. Her heart started reaching out to him, the need for comfort, for contact intensifying.

"Just one of the mysteries of the disorder," she muttered. She couldn't accept comfort from Alex. That would be overstepping a boundary she would never cross. He was Alex, and he had a vested interest in her as a dancer, not in her emotions.

She sighed, turned to him. "It's late. You've been here so long, thanks. I really appreciate—"

"Hold it – hold it." He stood before her with restless hands on his hips and a look of irritation on his face. "You've been through something huge today, and I'm not about to walk out of here and leave you alone."

"I am alone, Alex. Look around. Do you see a husband? I don't need you or anyone to take care of me. I've been taking care of myself for three years now."

"And doing a damned good job. I can see that." Frustrated, he ran a hand through his hair after a sigh. "But—" How could he tell her that he wasn't ready to leave yet? That he sensed she needed someone, and he wanted to be there for her to cry on, scream at, whatever.

Along with that need, he could tell she was holding back, like a dam gorged with water. "Let me make you something to eat," he offered. "You've got to be hungry."

"I'm not." Though her stomach was hollow, she really just wanted to fall on the couch and sleep. As if he read her thoughts, he gently took her shoulders and led her over, easing her into it.

"Toast, at least." He didn't look to see if she agreed, just went into her kitchen. It was white and blue, with damask curtains pulled back. Blue plates from Copenhagen hung in a scattered pattern on one wall, black and white snapshots of Paris on another.

Clean and orderly, it was vacant of a lot of cluttering knick-knacks. He kept his bread in the refrigerator so he looked there first. He smiled when he saw that she bought the same brand he did – whole wheat, organic.

With that svelte body of hers, she probably didn't eat toast with butter, but he popped his head back into the living room to ask. "Butter?"

She shook her head.

It felt good caring for her. He wasn't a stranger to caring for others, a fact he was sure few people knew. Experience had taught him that love made anyone capable.

He scoffed as the toast popped up. To be thinking about Lauren and love in the same sentence was jumping way ahead. Still, what had kept him at her side through this afternoon's ordeal was more than just his financial interest in her. That he could not ignore. Though he wasn't ashamed to admit his heart pulled and twisted whenever he looked at her, he'd been through enough women to know that alone wasn't enough to keep his interest either.

He'd been crazy with jealousy when she left the studio, telling him that she was seeing someone else. He wondered why she didn't call the man – tell him what happened? Anybody that cared about her would want to know. Was their relationship so advanced that they would talk about it as they both lay in bed, sharing their last wakeful thoughts in an intimate gesture of goodnight?

Those same jealous sparks flew through him again, and he let out a deep sigh. That was something he would have to find out, and if it were true, he would have to change it.

She was staring off into nothing, looking, he thought, utterly wasted – a mother wrung and left parched. He took the plate of toast and handed it to her.

"Thanks." She smiled at him as she took the plate.

"Is there anyone you'd like me to call for you – your parents, Rebekah's dad? Anybody?" He couldn't bring himself to add, your *boyfriend*.

She shook her head with a bitter laugh. "Yeah, right. Peter's been gone for three years. And there's no sense worrying my parents. My mom would just fly out here thinking that by *being* here she could have prevented it somehow."

Alex wanted to know about the man in her life.

Where was the goon now when she needed him? But Lauren really didn't need a man in her life. If anything, she needed convincing she didn't have to be so independent. Most men wanted to feel needed, and he was no exception, though he prized a woman with her own agenda. Lauren's life was huge, an uncharted atlas she was trying to navigate.

"You're worried about her." He sat in one of the floral, stuffed chairs that faced the solid denim blue couch.

She nodded, took a bite of the toast. "I can't have this happen again. It's too…my stomach – it will take days for it to settle down. If anything had happened to her…"

Feeling the weight of what she carried like a boulder across his own back, he nodded. But he didn't know what to say to ease her suffering. He wasn't a parent, hadn't even spent much time imagining himself as a father. He couldn't begin to pretend he understood how it felt to have a handicapped child.

"She doesn't understand anything about safety innately. Even if I took her to the door and told her, *now don't run because you'll get lost. There will be cars that could hit you, dogs that might bite, people that could hurt you*…she'd never get that."

"What does she understand?"

She lifted a shoulder. "It's hard to say at this point. Sometimes, I think she gets a lot of what's going on around her, but she's just too over stimulated by her environment and she tunes out. Then there are times when I can tell she's completely out of it. I could be screaming right in her face, and she wouldn't see or hear me."

He shook his head, marveling. "Sounds unbelievably frustrating."

"I don't know how much you know about autism." She

bit into the toast again.

"Not much – you know, "Rain Man" is about it. And I gather that's a one in a million case."

"It's not the norm," she told him after a swallow. "But then using autism and norm in the same breath is a bit of an oxymoron. I must sound sour. Sorry, but sometimes I really resent what fate's dealt me."

"You don't have to apologize. You're entitled. I think you're handling it very well, actually."

"Yeah, well, I have my days, just like everyone else. Today was not one of my better ones." She set the empty plate aside and wiped her hands together.

Anxious to do something, he rubbed his fingers back and forth. "How about an alarm? My parents' have one and every time a door or window opens, it makes a little sound. That might alert you to her movements."

Before, she hadn't been able to afford it, though she heard a lot of parents handled runaways the same way. Her mother antenna would get a chance to relax, knowing she would hear any possible attempt to run. It would be costly, but the peace of mind would be worth it.

It was so unfair she had to live like this, she thought, perilously close to being sucked into the voracious tornado of self-pity. Would she ever be able to leave a window open and enjoy a casual breeze ever again? Window screens weren't enough of a barrier, that was common knowledge. It sounded so ridiculous, but realities and freedoms other people enjoyed were not always hers.

"How about it?" Alex asked.

"It would probably help." She rose, took her plate into the kitchen and heard him behind her. To have someone there listening, suggesting, helping, was not something she was used to, and she knew then how easy it could be to like it.

She couldn't allow herself to. She faced him with her hand out, as she had learned since childhood from dance to end every social interaction. "Thanks for everything."

At first he stared at her hand, then looked into her eyes. "This is it?"

"Well, what do you expect? Look, I appreciate that you were here, I really do, but it's getting late and I'm bushed."

His face twisted into a quirked look of annoyance. "You're an honest little bunny, I'll give you that."

"Bunny?" She stood more erect, her head cocked. "And just what were you hoping for? That my unfortunate events would have me falling into your arms? I've been living with this for three years now, and I haven't needed to fall into anybody's arms yet."

"Now wait a second—"

"No, you wait a second. You see every woman as a plaything, Alex. What, did you come willing to help because you thought I'd like it? That it might strike points for you?"

"What are you talking about?" He thrust his hands through his hair on a groan. "You are so off base here."

"If I'm so off base, why are you getting angry about it? You always did get angry when the truth was involved."

His fingers dug restlessly into his hair, leaving it mussed. His eyes blackened as they bore into hers. "You're wrong."

She stepped toward him, mirroring his stance. "I don't believe you," she said. Her insides were ablaze. Any weariness fled, leaving flames now ready to devour anything in their path. "In fact, here's what I think. I think this whole sponsorship thing is just a big joke – a front. For what, I'm sure you'll take great pleasure in showing me. You've hated me since we were kids. Why, I've never been able to figure out. I cared then, when I was young, easily frightened by the big senior. Maybe that was why you couldn't stand me, because I didn't worship you like everybody else. It doesn't matter now, because I'm not a little girl. I can fight back, and if you don't think I will, then think again."

He wanted to snatch her, to smash her body mercilessly into his. His fingers damned near twitched with the need to tear into her, smother her mouth, silence her lies and force her into submission, see just how long she fought before melting into the heat he knew they could create together.

Unfortunately for him, touching her right at that moment would mean certain death – for him. Facial scratches to be sure. He wouldn't even put it past her to lamb him in the balls. While he wasn't used to backing away from a challenge, he wasn't stupid enough to take chances. He didn't want her to hate him any more than she already did. That humbling, horrific thought caused him to take a step back.

She was right, he was used to women who agreed with him for the sake of it. He'd grown used to the predictability. Maturing had left him gravitating toward women with spunk. Not just any woman with spunk, for each relationship had left him only wondering about her.

He still wondered – that was his problem. Which made her right about the fact that he had approached the sponsorship with ulterior motives. He could tuck his tail between his legs and leave with some dignity, he thought then. She'd seen right through him, and the revelation was like being naked, without the hope of perks.

But then turnabout was fair play. That he knew, that he

would enjoy. He stepped toward her, feeling the heat of her anger fade a little. "Guess what, babe; I've known all along that **you've been curious about me. That's the truth.**" He nodded, satisfied when those green eyes of her flashed. "That's right. You loved to tease me. You knew it got under my skin and you did it anyway…blatantly, I might add." Slowly, he inched his face to hers, glad she didn't back away, furious that he couldn't do what he wanted to her. "And you liked it just as much as I liked it."

Her nervous tongue wet her lips, and his heated gaze flicked there.

"So why do you do it?" he asked. "If you know it gets to me, you must do it because you want to."

When they were kids, she meant to antagonize him, get back at him. But they were adults now. The sport was real and the stakes were much more dangerous because they were both consenting to the game.

For a flash, he debated taking that will of hers and crushing it beneath hands and lips capable of extinguishing it for the sake of conquering her. His conscience wouldn't let him. He reminded himself that her daughter slept not fifteen feet away. She'd been through hell and back. She looked like a warrior who'd already been in battle but still stood with her spear ready.

Sudden compassion washed away any desire to fight with her and he let out a sigh, lowering his head. "I'm sorry." Though he was not prepared to apologize for the argument, the words spilled out. He lifted his eyes to hers. "It is late, you're right. I should go before we both say things we'll regret."

"I haven't said anything but the truth," she told him. He was surprised at the fight still in her tone.

"Truth according to you," he replied calmly. He turned, totally mystified that every time they were together it seemed to end in battle.

At the door, he looked back at her. She had not followed like most women would, expecting something more from him. She was all but ready to boot his butt out the door. But her shoulders drooped just enough that he knew the day had finally caught up with her. As he left, his only thought was that he wished he could wrap his arms around her and ease some of her suffering.

eleven

Rebekah was safely on the bus for another day of school, and Lauren stood on the sidewalk watching. The aide helped Rebekah into her seat, strapped the belt around her, and Rebekah looked off into some place Lauren would probably never see. Rebekah rarely ever looked back at her. Today was no different.

Lauren walked nearer to the bus, trying to catch Rebekah's attention with a wave. Her daughter's angelic face finally turned and her blue eyes, usually distracted by things of mystery, found Lauren's.

Another little victory she could tuck inside. Rebekah stared blankly at her as the bus pulled away from the curb. Lauren's heart snagged. She felt pretty sure Rebekah knew she was on the bus going for another day at school. It had been hardest that first day, sending her child off knowing her baby had no idea what was going on except that she was going for a ride somewhere with people she didn't know.

Explaining only soothed Lauren, for Rebekah just boarded the bus with innocent faith and trust. The heavy responsibility of protecting and taking care of her grew each time Lauren trusted others with her.

In a world fraught with injustice, cruelty, and people lying in wait to take advantage, Lauren first thought she would home school, Rebekah's vulnerabilities an ocean she was trying to hold back with human hands. Impossible as that was, she slowly realized there were good people who loved those less fortunate, even if her own family proved incapable. Even with a husband who never would love his own daughter.

Often Lauren pondered her defensive stance and finally attributed its roots to people like Alex and Peter. People who were mean for no other reason but to be mean. In Peter's case, he just didn't have the courage to deal with what God gave him. It wasn't fair that people like Peter ran when something got tough, or those crossed wood beam appeared on the horizon. Equally unfair were those who had it all, like Alex, sitting in some mansion somewhere cutting money like cards in a deck. Because life made her defensive first, optimistic second, Lauren knew the effort it took to not let pessimism get the best of her.

Alex hit the nail on the head saying she deliberately provoked him. She thought it was cute in fact, that he'd asked her why. She could have told him. But that would end his misery, and that wouldn't be any fun at all.

As she walked back into the house, she noticed the grass needed mowing, the flowerbeds weeding. How long had it been since she'd had the crabgrass? Hadn't she paid a lawn service for a preventative spray? She couldn't remember. Like all things mundane, her brain seemed only to allow for things vital – Rebekah, her students, her income, and her career with Chad. Everything else came and went with the frivolity of a perfumed scent one enjoys for a moment, then forgets as it fades.

Today she would call an alarm company and look into the cost of installation. If she had to be there through the job it could take away from her students, something she couldn't allow. Her classes were packed and parents got uptight if their students didn't get what they paid for.

Stage parents were a nightmare, loitering around the

edge of the dance floor, screaming at children to do better, listen more and quit messing around. Maybe it was because her daughter would never do the amazing things her students did, but Lauren never ceased to marvel at the little bodies when they twisted, turned and dipped in the difficult steps of cha-cha or hopped with never-ending energy to the demands of jive. Why didn't these parents just sit back and enjoy the amazing feats their children could accomplish?

The phone rang, and she picked it up in the kitchen, her eyes lighting now on the plate with crumbs Alex had brought to her the night before.

"Hello?"

"Lauren, it's Alex."

"Alex. Hi."

"Listen, I called BTA and they're going to come out and install whatever you want. I told them cost didn't matter, that you needed Fort Knox. They should be calling you for an install date this morning. They can do it any time this week. I thought it might help to ease your concerns if you didn't have to worry about it."

Her first thought was to scream at him. Her defenses flew up like a cobra ready to strike. Even as her blood simmered, she knew better. He was trying to help, a fact she appreciated; a deed she would take even if pride demanded otherwise.

"That was thoughtful. Thank you."

"You're welcome. I could see how worried you were, and I know how busy you are. So, I thought I'd get the ball rolling."

"Again, I thank you. But it really wasn't necessary."

He paused. "Okay," he said slowly. "I sense a thunder storm."

"Alex, I have fingers, I can dial a phone. I have a voice. I can speak for myself. I have money; I can pay for my own needs."

"Don't flip out, Lauren." She could hear his voice draw tight. "I just thought with everything that had happened, you might want some—"

"I'm not flipping out. I just don't want to feel like I owe you."

"Because I called the alarm place you feel like you owe me?"

"You paid for it, Alex. How is that supposed to make me feel if not indebted? But then that's what you want, isn't it? You want to own me, that's the bottom line here."

He grunted into the phone, and a shudder ran through her heart and trembled into her belly.

"What is it with you?" he was very near a growl. "Is it that you can't accept help, or you just won't accept it from me?"

"Yes to both of those," she snapped, "but an especially big yes to the second because with you there are attachments."

"What freaking attachments? Have I asked you to do anything against your will?"

She had to lift the phone from her ear for a moment. The picture of him pressing her against the door of her car flashed into her mind and along with it the hot sparks she felt when he had. "Do you get some sort of kick out of hearing me tell you? Like some twisted form of reinforcement?"

For a moment she didn't hear anything but heavy silence and thick breathing. An old fear fluttered in her belly, a fear she hadn't felt since she had seen him coming toward her in the mass of students walking down the hall in junior high, and she'd darted another direction just to avoid him.

He was on the phone now, and she was in no danger of running into him – except later at rehearsal. She didn't want to damage their sponsorship and knew she was close to truly alienating him, so she said, "I'm sorry. I'll thank you for your help again. But in the future, please ask me. Don't jump to conclusions about me. You don't know me, Alex. You don't really know me at all."

Still, he said nothing. She wondered if she'd finally pushed too many buttons at once. She expected him to tell her to jump off a cliff with her car wrapped around her throat. He could hang up on her. She'd been rude, and she would take that. What she feared most, what made her tremble with anticipation both thrilling and frightening was what he told her next.

"I'll see you at rehearsal, Lauren." His voice was the hot steel of a blade that promised a deep cut. The click following was sharp with disapproval, and she slowly set the phone into the receiver, her body buzzing with anticipation.

twelve

Before rehearsal, Alex stopped by his parents' house. He'd moved out years ago, but as their only child, knew they expected regular visits. And after his father's accident, his mother had made it glaringly obvious that she needed his support.

He pulled up in front of the Verdi electric gates at the bottom of the drive and pressed the code into the security box, then watched the gates slowly open. The house wasn't visible from the quiet street, where other large homes lined the curved, tree-laden road. But it was the Saunders' home that got all of the attention.

There were few houses this size in Pleasant Grove and their neighborhood, just at the foot of majestic and towering Mount Timpanogos, was where a handful of estates had been erected. There was safety and acceptance in like numbers, he mused driving up the sandstone drive. His parents had taught him that from the beginning.

It was necessary to remove yourself in some things, they had said, when money is involved. People just don't see you as their equal. Alex had come to understand that from the very beginning.

He parked his car and locked the doors with the click of his remote. Rodriguez was raking leaves on one of the large expanses of grass, and Alex waved at him. The Latino man and his crew had been working for his parents for as long as he could recall.

He'd even taught Alex basic Spanish one summer. It was

Alex's mother's belief that though her son came from money, a little hard labor would round out gratitude very nicely. So Alex worked along side the Latino crew every summer during junior high. After he'd turned sixteen, he'd gotten a job at a nearby grocery store.

Alex never entered the house through the large, heavy glass front doors. He used the back entrance. There he pushed in another code, and waited for the beep before he could enter.

The alarm reminded him of Lauren and their conversation. His body hummed thinking about the fight in her voice. Her raw independence got to him in a way that he appreciated. That fight, so edgy, so ready, definitely provoked him.

He checked his watch, counting down until seven. He couldn't wait to see her and give her a piece or two of his mind, ripe as it was becoming. Too bad Chad would have to be there, he mused, tossing his keys on the black granite kitchen counter top. The possibilities would be endless, exciting and hot if they could only be alone.

"Mother?" he called out, sure he'd have to use the intercom to find her. The kitchen was wont of any odors. He knew she wasn't making dinner. She'd stopped what scant cooking she had done almost entirely when he'd moved out. His father only ate the equivalent of baby food. "Cooking for one is unfulfilling," she'd told him more than once. She'd left the responsibility to Margaret, their cook, who'd been with them since Alex was ten. His mother insisted that he eat with her on Sundays, and he honored that request whenever he could.

The nearest intercom was on the maple wood wall next to the built-in desk his mother used for writing letters and paying bills. He depressed the button on the intercom. "Mother? Where are you?"

Her voice crackled through the speaker. "Is that you?"

"Who else would it be?" he chided her. "Where are you?"

"In my office. Come up, I want to show you something."

Uh-oh. He broke out in an uncomfortable sweat and headed toward the back staircase. He took them two and a time. The scent of Estee Lauder perfume signaled to his senses she was indeed in her office.

He found her over her large worktable, her black hair pulled back and up in the practical yet tasteful knot of the ballet dancer she had once been. Her slim form was dressed as casual as he ever saw her. For Catherine Saunders, that wasn't anything less than a tailored pair of slacks in tan or some other neutral shade and a knit top in a high color she wore specifically to enhance the angled drama of her plum-like cheekbones and deep set eyes.

"Mother." He went right to her, knowing she expected a kiss, and pressed one to her cheek. Her signature perfume filled his senses, taking him to a flash of boyhood memories he couldn't distinguish but that warmed him all the same.

"Darling." She touched his elbow as he kissed her, then as he drew back her dark brown eyes – his eyes, he had been told – examined him the way only a mother's could – with the intent to uncover secrets and search for signs of ill health. "You look tired," she told him. "Didn't sleep well last night?"

He moved back a few inches, hoping to buy himself some protection from her inquisitive gaze but knew it was impossible. "I slept fine. How's Dad?"

"You can't change the subject that quickly, Alex.

Something's bothering you."

"Even if that were true, and it's not, I wouldn't tell you." He kissed her cheek again, trying to distract her. "What's all this?"

"Look what I found," she gushed, spreading elegant hands over the neatly laid out photos and supplies covering the table. Alex looked at the pictures – everywhere his face beamed, in color, black and white, in casual and in studio settings with all of the pomp of a celebrity.

"Yeah." He worked to muster interest over stronger feelings of embarrassment. She had already constructed fifteen three-inch leather albums of just him and that was outrageous enough. He was a teenager in these photos, years and memories that had often left him confused and angry after the accident.

"Look how adorable you were," she oozed with pride. She picked up a photo of him with the guys – the same guys he'd hung with the night he'd followed Lauren out to her car.

"Damian called the other day; did I tell you?" she said, eyeing the photo. He looked over her shoulder and gazed at it.

"Did he?"

"He wanted to know how your father was, and how to get in touch with you."

"You didn't say anything about—"

"Of course not," she scoffed. "He's started anew I imagine, and that's a good thing. You're men now, so I know I don't have any right to say, but if you were still boys I'd not let you anywhere near him."

"That's the mother in you talking." Alex scratched his jaw, wondering what his old friend wanted after all these years. They hadn't talked after that night. Both had come and gone through graduation without even a congratulatory handshake, then parted ways. That night of aggression against Lauren had been a part of Damian Alex had never seen. But it was only the beginning.

Alex looked at the smiling faces in the photo wondering if he'd ever hear from him or if it was just a passing attempt. He put the picture down, looked at his mother, still engrossed, smiling at the pictures.

"I'm going to go see Dad." He brushed her elbow with his fingers, but her eyes never left the photographs, she just nodded.

Alex walked down the long, empty hall that led him to the secluded part of the house his father and the help they hired for his care inhabited.

His father lay awake, his clear blue eyes staring off into nothing. He and Harold, one of the live-in nurses, watched the horse races on a large plasma TV hung strategically where George could see it as his head rested on a pillow.

Alex smiled at Harold who rose to shake his hand.

"Hey, Dad." Alex went right to his father's bedside. Slowly, George's head turned, and those light blue eyes met his.

"We've bet on 'She's the One' and 'Rough Ride' to place," Harold said.

With a glance at the screen, Alex nodded. His father's clear blue eyes looked more alert today, but then Alex knew how easy it was to see something because of hope.

"How you doing today, Dad?" Alex leaned close, waiting for any change on his father's face. "Hey, did I tell you I'm taking dancing lessons. Can you believe it? Me? You always liked to dance, didn't you? This woman who's teaching me is a champion ballroom dancer. In fact, I'm sponsoring her. You remember Chad Stehli, Bill and Stella Stehli's son? He dances with Lauren, this woman I'm seeing."

Was it his tender imagination, or did his father's open mouth look as if it was struggling into a smile. Alex's grip tightened around his father's arm, his gaze stayed fixed. Overhead, the television blared with the screams and applause of the winners of the race.

Alex would like nothing more than to think he could share part of his heart with his father. He'd dreamed it so often. Even thinking about how, as a boy, he'd wrapped his arms around him, weeping on his lifeless form, begging him to get better brought pain to his heart. He'd been sucked into depression and misery, consumed with all that he and his father would never do

"She's something else, Dad."

"You've met someone?" Harold asked with a grin.

Alex nodded. The years and his father had made them friends.

"He'll like that," Harold added.

"He'll love it." Alex turned again to his father. "I'll bring her by so you can meet her. I used to talk about her, but you may not remember. She's had me since junior high school. I fell for her way back then."

"George, should we pick again? Last time we didn't do too well," Harold said, looking at the line up on the screen for the next race.

"I'm on my way to dance with her, Dad," Alex leaned over, placed a soft kiss on his father's forehead then stayed close, blinking hard. "I'll see you on Sunday."

Alex left the room just as Harold recited the names of the horses running the next race. His heart was heavy, as it often was after visits. That feeling came and went now;

thankfully, it wasn't a permanent resident anymore. He'd shoved it out years ago when he'd decided to cling to hope and faith.

He found his mother cutting and pasting his smiling images into her latest work of art and kissed her cheek, then hung over her shoulder, looking into the faces of a boy that still lived somewhere inside of him.

"Leaving already, darling?"

"Have an appointment."

He knew she was too distracted to ask about it, and he wasn't sure he was ready to tell her about him and Lauren.

He went to the door.

"Sunday?" she asked, pressing a bright yellow, cut frame around a photo of him and Damian into the book.

"I'll be here." He turned to leave when she spoke again.

"Who is she, Alex?"

He stopped, poised in the door, and looked at her over his shoulder. She wore the slightest smile.

"Never could hide anything from you," he turned, and leaned in the jamb.

She settled back in her chair, eyes bright with curiosity. "Do tell."

Alex swallowed the tiny lump in his throat knowing his mother would never settle for a generic answer. "Her name is Lauren Peay."

Catherine's brow lifted. "The same Lauren Peay that you loved to hate back in junior high school?"

Alex shifted. "You knew about that?"

"Darling," Catherine's laugh fluttered. "You were crazy with it."

Alex's brows knit together. "Yeah, but I didn't know it

was obvious."

"I have been both mother and father, even though you rarely talked to me about such things. So she's back in your life. I trust that this time you are taking action and not just letting your interest in the woman fester." She gave him a tsk-tsk and arched a brow.

Alex shoved his hands in his front pockets and figured it was a good time to get out of there, before he discovered more embarrassing enlightenments.

With a humble kiss to his mother's cheek, Alex said goodbye and headed to the studio. Twenty minutes and he would see Lauren.

Driving, he pictured her as he'd first seen her in junior high school, the dark-haired beauty with a smile fresh as any girl he'd seen on the cover of one of his mother's fashion magazines. As if she didn't have a care or worry in the world, she had breezed through the halls with her sweet and timid little girlfriends like a flock of baby ducks – or bunnies, as he'd called them – irresistible to a fox hungry for that same untroubled existence.

He parked next to her car, glad she was already there. Unfortunately, Chad's car was also in the parking lot, which meant any private interaction would have to wait until after rehearsal.

Retrieving the portfolio with the costume designs, he headed down the stairs to the lower studio.

thirteen

She wore black. The slick fabric clung to every long, taut muscle like eager skin, with just enough sheen that when she arched, swayed and twisted, Alex's blood rushed and spun.

He wet his lips and stood with his arms across his chest just at the edge of where she and Chad were being coached by Reuben. Alex watched her every move of the demanding contractions from her thighs and buttocks, amazed at the elegant bend of her back. Every motion was pure and perfect, moving to the music as if each fiber in her body was in tune with the beat.

Alex had a lot to learn when it came to dance, and he intended to learn all that he could – from her. Lauren didn't know it yet, but she was going to teach him those magical moves because he'd be damned if he was going to stand by and watch other men touch her that way.

Just thinking about feeling her body move against his stirred him, and he wet his lips again, shifting his stance. Not being able to dance with her left him feeling chained to a wall when a sumptuous meal lay just out of his reach. If his life circumstances had taught him one thing, it was that he could break any barrier and do anything he put his mind to.

He tried to understand Reuben's corrections, watched carefully when Reuben demonstrated moves, filing the information away in his mind. When it was his turn to learn, he wanted to impress, to shock Lauren's beautiful eyes a deeper shade of green.

She'd only glanced at him when he first entered and that

wasn't enough. His blood was bubbling in fact that she didn't make more effort to schmooze and kiss up. She owed it to him – he was her financial lifeline now. Then he wanted to back up and kick himself for thinking that way. Hadn't she just accused him of this very thing? And hadn't he adamantly denied it, even though it was true?

He'd keep on denying it until she submitted. Until she was his, he'd pretend that he wasn't after her as if his next breath depended on it.

"Let's take a five minute break," Reuben told Lauren and Chad. Alex barely felt the sigh that escaped him then. Try as he may to appear as though he didn't want to leap across the studio and snag her attention, he couldn't stop his heart from thundering when she looked at him.

He took it as an invitation and crossed to her, the portfolio tucked under his arm.

"How's Rebekah?" he asked, noticing that she looked rested despite the sweat of hard work.

"Good." She wiped her forehead with the hem of her long-sleeved black shirt and started toward a chair where her duffle sat. He stayed at her side, sending a cordial wave to Reuben and Chad, deep in conversation.

She unzipped the duffle, rifled through it. "The alarm will be installed tomorrow." She pulled out a water bottle and opened it.

"Good." He wanted to ask her if she was still mad at him but got caught up in the tilt of her head, the light sheen covering her throat as she swallowed the water. He wanted to run eager fingers along that very place.

He flipped open the portfolio and her sketched image lay before them. He liked that she stopped drinking, that her movements slowed. She stared at herself in blood red with silver sequins and fringe. The first dress was spectacular, and would imprison the judges' eyes if for no other reason but that she looked sensational. That would matter to her, he was sure, but not as much as functionality and her skills as a dancer would matter.

"What do you think?" he asked.

She screwed the blue top on her water bottle. "Let's see Chad's."

He didn't like that she hadn't flipped over the dress and felt his jaw tighten as he turned the page. Chad's costume mirrored hers, with the same high color and dramatic placement of sequins and fringe. Together, they would be showstoppers.

"What else do you have?" she asked. Alex wanted to slap the portfolio shut, but he went on to the next design, these in oceanic blue. The dress was a halter style with the back cut low, the skirt flirty, flaring mid thigh. She'd look hot in that one as well, he thought, staring at the sketch of her long legs poised apart, one bent, the other pointed. To smell her and feel her next to him, yet be staring at her image in colored pencil was an odd experience, sending his nerves into a skip.

There were three designs in all, the ruby, the sapphire and one for the elegant dances of standard done in heavenly white with a long, flowing skirt dusted in sparkling rhinestones. She finally looked up at him.

"They'll do," she said and turned to cross back to the center of the floor where Reuben and Chad waited to resume rehearsing. He snagged her arm.

"They'll do?"

Her eyes flickered with challenge. It drove the skip inside

of him into a fast run. He let her go, but she didn't move, she just lifted her chin. His breath was coming in fast. Hers was faster, as if they'd both sprinted around a track. If he didn't kiss her soon, he'd careen off that path and run himself into hell.

She left him then, and the swing in her hips told him she knew he was watching her. It was bittersweet, the power women held over men. And he hated that he liked it, torturous as it was to his system. He figured the battering would be worth it, once he had her all to himself.

But he was miles away from that and the very distance of it ate at him. He paced out of the realm where Reuben pushed them back into another long, sweaty rehearsal.

Like a lion shunned from the kill, he stayed back, watching the three of them work. His need to learn intensified. It wasn't that he wanted to compete, though he knew if he so chose to undertake such an endeavor, he could. It was where Lauren was at, and he wanted to be there with her.

After Reuben was satisfied with the rehearsal, he and Chad looked over the designs, casting their votes for the blue ensembles.

"They're sizzlin'," Reuben let out a whistle. "Doubt anybody'll be watching your form when you wear that."

Alex watched Lauren guardedly to see if she would finally show some emotion over the dress one way or the other, but she remained annoyingly passive.

"You done good, man." Reuben patted Alex on the shoulder. "Those costumes are some of the best I've seen. Excellent work."

"Thank you." Alex smiled, relieved even more so when Reuben and Chad gathered their things and headed out the door. At last, he and Lauren would be alone.

When the heavy door finally shut with a thud, he turned and looked at her. He knew she'd been teaching for two hours before that grueling practice he'd just witnessed, but he wanted more, and he crossed to her.

Coming to a stop just close enough to catch that her floral perfume had washed away some with sweat and hard work, he stuffed hands anxious to touch her deep into his front pockets. "I want to ask you something," he started.

She tilted her head up at him, reaching for her sweater. His hand was out in a snap, covering hers, stopping her from donning the sweater. Confused by his action, her eyes sharpened on his.

"I want you to teach me to dance."

Her chin lifted with that female power she knew she held over him, something he couldn't take away because the truth of it was too enticing. He wanted her to teach him, yes, but if pride were going to stand in the way, he'd find some other way to learn.

"What about Chad?" she asked, the glitter of challenge alive in her eyes.

"I want to dance with a woman, thank you." One, in particular, he thought but wouldn't say.

"I can't."

"Why not?"

She slipped one arm into her sweater. "It would be a mistake, Alex."

"Tell me how teaching me something you teach to other people would be a mistake."

"You're my sponsor." She put her other arm in, started buttoning. "It would be a conflict of interest."

He rammed his hands through his hair and spun around

before facing her like a bull ready to attack a matador.

"Easy, easy," she said then, her head tilting at him with just a hint of pleasure in her green eyes. It shot his system into a hot swirl of frustration. "Why do you want to dance?" she asked, crossing her arms.

There was no way he was going to tell her that he wanted to be her equal in a place she was far superior to him, or that he wanted to hold her body against his, feel it tease and tempt. He wouldn't tell her it was the only way he could spend the time he wanted to spend with her, under the guise of learning.

"Can't a guy that has everything pick one more thing?" he shrugged.

She snatched her duffle. "You're impossible, you know that?"

In a flash, he was tugging the duffle from her grasp. "How about if I told you I'm not asking."

Her eyes slit. "You mean you expect it? With our arrangement and all, you expect me to teach you?"

He nodded, readying for the next round.

With the calculated finesse of a stripper, she peeled off her sweater and set it on the chair. He thought his heart would flip right out of his chest. There was iciness on her shoulders, erect as they now were, but he didn't care if he got frostbitten, he had to dance with her.

"Sure," she said. Then she left him, went to the very center of the room, turned, and waited.

fourteen

So he wanted her to teach him how to dance? Lauren couldn't believe he hadn't respected her answer; rather he'd taken her decision and sent it flying out the window for the sake of usurping his power.

But he owned her now, and she shouldn't be surprised that he would demand things. Her heart fluttered. What else would he demand? Dance she could handle, she would simply treat him as any other student. Though she had been forced to accept the offer to have the alarm system installed, that was a necessity she could overlook eventually.

He came toward her and a delicious slither of the unknown traveled from her lips to her center, filling her with heat that tingled and spread, gliding slippery, fast and sweet.

He was dressed in jeans today, a sight she hadn't seen since high school. They weren't ordinary jeans, these had been designed to hold his body alone. Black was a color he wore well and often. She figured he must like knit shirts because they fit like a comfortable caress, showing just enough to stir blood.

He pushed up his sleeves as he drew closer, and she purposefully kept her gaze steady so as to not give away the heat slowly building inside of her.

"Correct me if I'm wrong," she started, holding her arms up in ready position. "But you were interested in learning the rumba."

"Oh, you can bet I'll correct you if you're wrong." He set his left hand in her right, placed his right hand at the tight curve of her waist.

"Of course you will," she said.

"But it's the tango I want you to teach me now." Alex enjoyed that her head tilted in surprise. "*International tango.*" He'd been doing research. Had watched half a dozen of her taped competitions he'd talked out of Chad, and realized while rumba was hot to watch, it was tango where the dancer's bodies fused unbreakably.

"International tango it will be then, boss." He didn't like the sound of that and frowned. "Something wrong?" she asked.

"Look, there's no conflict of interest with us dancing because we're not dancing. I'm so far from dancing I'm in another state. You're a teacher and I'm a student. No conflict, see?"

"Oh," her sarcasm was light. "That makes it totally clear to me – thanks. In tango, the hips are together, the body is positioned close, like this," she began and settled herself right up against him. This was not some little boy like she was used to teaching, and his complete maleness shot sparks through her whether she liked it or not.

His whole body was toned and masculine and every soft and female part of her fit too nicely into the curves God had created just for her. Sweat that had dried minutes ago sprung forth in jubilation down her back, along her forehead, in her palms.

"Very good," she told him, but didn't dare look up into his eyes. "The dance position in tango is different than any other standard dance. It's tighter, more compact. Your hand should go here," she said, lifting his hand and pulling it around her back, at the same time placing her left hand underneath his arm, fusing both of their arms together. "You're not supporting me with the palm of your hand: our bodies are joined here, at the center, and that is where the support comes from."

"I see," he shifted, and the slight movement was like a cat had just nestled comfortably against her. She felt the splendid security of it from her chest to her thighs.

She cleared her throat. "This is the beginning stance." Sweat poured in rivulets down her back, under her breasts. She took the opportunity to ease out of his arms and step back, everything jittering as she scrambled with what to do to control her reaction to him. She turned, giving him her back so she could demonstrate.

"The man's part goes like this – your legs are slightly bent as you step." She then began the slow, forward walk of promenade with her hands up, holding an invisible partner. "Slow, slow, quick, quick. Slow, slow, quick, quick," she counted, and with one glance over her shoulder could see that he was following along.

So attuned to complimenting her young students she couldn't stop the compliments that tumbled from her then: "Excellent. Very good." She stopped herself when she saw his face break into a proud smile.

She stood back, and he stopped. "Keep going," she snapped. If she was the teacher, he was going to feel it, she decided then, relishing that she could, and would, tell him what to do and he'd have to do it – no questions asked.

"That's your basic walk and link, usually it leads to promenade. Keep going, all around the room."

"Without you?"

"Yup," she nodded, smiled as he continued around in a amazingly accurate circle. Could he possibly be great at every single thing he did?

Finally his circling brought him back to her. He stopped,

placing his hands on his hips. "What next?"

"You haven't perfected that yet, Fred."

"Fred?"

"Astair." She gestured for him to keep going but he slid next to her and suddenly her body was pressing into that severe maleness she was trying in vain to avoid.

"Let's try it together." His brown eyes glittered.

"The teacher doesn't dance with her students."

"Forget that, babe," he grinned. "I've seen you and you're lying through those pretty teeth of yours."

She had to laugh at that. It seemed to break the tight string of enmity that invisibly strung them together. "All right then, on my count." She began counting and they moved.

"Slowly, Alex. You're moving too fast. But then I'm sure you've heard that before." She cocked a brow at him.

Concentration tightened his striking features. She enjoyed stealing glimpses as his thoughts took him to a place in dance she knew very well herself. He was starting to perspire; tiny beads sprung at his hairline, a light sheen made the skin of his neck and throat glisten. The heat in his body had risen with the exertion. His shirt would be damp soon and a pleasant shudder went straight to her middle anticipating what it would do to his chest when the fabric clung.

He was amazingly cooperative, even as she made him go over and over specific steps. His patience seemed endless, and that impressed her. She had assumed he was little more than an active volcano ready to blow at any moment. He'd been volatile for as long as she'd known him.

So involved had she been in his speedy progress and the fun back and forth repartee, she didn't noticed that time had gotten away from her. She gasped when she finally checked the clock hanging over the door.

"I'm forty-minutes late!" In a dash she was at the chair where her personal belongings sat waiting for her. She yanked on her sweater, tossed her duffle over her shoulder.

"Hey, hey." Alex was at her side. He tucked the portfolio under his arm. "I'll walk you out. It's dark out there." He didn't like that this particular studio at Center Stage faced a deserted alleyway right next to the freeway. Any goon could come along searching for an opportunity, and he didn't want it to be her.

"That's not necessary." She hurriedly flicked off the rows of overhead lights.

Holding the door open for her, Alex waited as she got the last light. "I insist. Do you work a lot of late nights?"

"Not with the children. Their classes all end at eight. But Chad and I sometimes work until eleven, if I can get Aubrey to take care of Rebekah."

"He walks you out, right?"

She glanced up at him. "Sometimes."

"He needs some lessons in manners."

"I've told you, I can take care of myself." She pulled the door shut and locked it with an industrial-sized key while he watched.

Still, Alex would make sure Chad was there for her, if he couldn't be.

"Thanks," he said as she passed. She looked up at him. It wasn't the right time to kiss her, not with the searing noise of cars speeding on the freeway less than one hundred feet away. There was nothing romantic about the creepy, lamely lit alley in which they now stood. But at the end of the alley was an opening, in the same way he could see an opening for them both. For an hour they had participated in something together and not argued. In Alex's book, there was hope.

fifteen

The alarm was supposed to be installed today, and the deep sense of relief Lauren anticipated was as near to the warm blanket of security as she'd gotten in years. She couldn't wait to wrap herself in it. She cleaned, waiting for the installers to arrive.

Growing up with a sister and a brother, she'd done her share of picking up. But she also knew that most children obeyed their parents and with enough encouragement, would eventually pick up on their own.

She doubted she would ever enjoy that luxury with Rebekah. Her three-year-old mind was like a garden of flowers, her capabilities coming in randomly, and all at various stages of development. Where Rebekah was physically capable to do the chore, mentally, she would not be able to understand such concepts as cleanliness and order.

"So I'm destined to pick up forever," Lauren said to herself, gathering Rebekah's scattered books and toys. Sometimes it miffed her that her family was spread out. That no one was around to help but a girl she'd had to hire.

At least her family made efforts to see Rebekah and her occasionally. Unlike Peter's parents who had taken the low road along with Peter distancing themselves from the harsh reality of Rebekah's condition.

For Lauren her life was her child, and though she didn't like to think about the very real fact that she may never share her life with anyone else because of that, Rebekah's care came first.

Men were a complication anyway, she thought now, checking her watch, wondering where the installers were. That brought her mind to Alex.

It still prickled her to think that he'd taken the reins out of her hands and arranged this whole alarm system thing. Nice as it was, comforting as she knew it would be, the defensive reaction always ready to burst whenever she and Alex were within five feet of each other had become as expected as the daily mail delivery.

Men were more than distractions, she thought, tidying the top of Rebekah's dresser. They were annoyances.

On the dresser was a white piece of paper with Rebekah's name in huge, erratic letters printed across it. Lauren picked it up and smiled. It was the first time Rebekah had written her name, with hand-over-hand help of her teacher. It was worth pinning on the wall. She scrounged for a thumbtack and placed it on a wall in the kitchen just as the doorbell rang.

When she opened the door, the face looking back at her wore a smile; but it was the eyes underneath the navy striped hat marked with BTA that had her scrutinizing the man.

"BTA," he started. "I'm here to install—" he was studying her as well, his dark eyes skittering her face like a rat chasing a crumb in the breeze. His grin spread slow and lazy. "Well, well, well. Lauren Peay."

It was then that she remembered, then that she could see fragments of a boy who'd perched himself over her that frightening night in the parking lot with the intent to do more than just give her a good scare. A shudder wracked her spine, and she swallowed the memory. That was years ago, she told herself. We're adults now. For crying out loud he's in the security business.

"Damian." She forced a smile. He leaned casually in her doorway as if he were her latest fling come to take her out for a pleasant lunch.

She took a moment to look at him. For a guy of thirty, he looked ragged and much older. The scent of cigarette socked her in the nose and by the bulge in the breast pocket of his uniform she figured he must have taken up the disgusting habit. His blue eyes were alive and sparkled with danger, just like she remembered them.

Slamming the door on his face would have been rude, and an overreaction, she told herself, so she stood back and let him enter.

"You're installing security systems now?" Her tone held the irony she saw in the situation. He seemed to get it, because his grin was still there, just like the danger in his eyes.

He passed her with a nod, looking her over like a man buying companionship for the evening. "Sure am. Wow, you look great."

She shut the door and faced him, making sure no trace of alarm shown on her face even though uncertainty whirled inside of her. "Thank you." It would be best to just let him get to work, to ignore what had happened all those years ago and keep distance. That and she would keep her cell phone on her hip in case she had to dial the police.

Maybe I'm way out of line, she thought, watching him look around. He looked clean, even if he stunk to high heaven of smoke. His hair was short and his uniform was neat and pressed. That had to count for something.

"So, how long have you been working for BTA?" she asked.

His gaze swept every corner and cranny of the room, but

finally landed on her. His eyes had that hungry look that sent another shudder of insecurity through her. "About four months now."

That wasn't enough time for loyalty or anything else to develop between employer and employee. Still, if Alex had known, Lauren figured it must be okay. He'd arranged for the installation. But she really didn't know if Alex and Damian's friendship had extended beyond high school.

Damian put down his thick, steel brief case and set his hands on his hips. "How about you? What have you been up to? I heard you were a dancer. I mean, you always danced, that I remember very well, but I heard you're a pro now."

More at ease talking about dance, Lauren tried to move casually around the room. "Yes. I compete in ballroom."

"Like waltz and stuff."

She nodded. "I also teach."

"Yeah, I'd heard that," he rubbed his chin. "At Center Stage, right?"

"You've heard of it?"

"Oh, yeah, my little girl used to take classes there."

Instantly the air of accusation seeped from her system. "You have a little girl?"

"Got married right after high school, but we're divorced now. Yeah, I took her there myself once or twice. She took ballet. Good program."

See, he has changed, she told herself, smiling at him. He'd grown up, just like the rest of them, had a child, made something of himself. With the revelation, she began to ease a little bit more.

He looked around again. "So this is your place. Wow, what a coincidence. I've wondered about you."

"You have?"

"Yeah, you know, after what happened that night. I was an idiot to say the least."

"You were," she said without hesitation. The faintest flickering in his eyes made her wonder if she shouldn't have been so honest. But they'd all changed, and she wasn't some weak female who wouldn't say what was on her mind. She never had been. "But that was a long time ago."

"Right," he said. "Well, guess I'll get started. Don't let me get in your way."

"I won't," she said. "What will you be doing, exactly?"

"Oh, I'll be installing a control panel say," he looked around, his eyes focused on the wall next to the door, "right there, so that when you come in, you can punch in your code and stuff. Set the alarm every time you come and go. Then I'll be drilling battery-run receptors to each window and door. The frequency will register at the panel when a door or window opens. You'll be able to see which one it is and if the alarm goes off when you're not home, because of an intruder, it will register at the office."

"So there's somebody watching twenty-four hours a day?" she asked.

He angled his head at her. "Absolutely."

Why that didn't reassure her, bugged her. He was the security expert after all. Maybe that was it, the strangeness of it all. Having some guy who'd scared the tar out of her now creating her mode of protection.

He was mostly quiet while he worked, but for the occasional whistle of some tunes Lauren didn't recognize. As she continued to clean, she kept a watchful if not curious eye on him forcing herself to smile if their eyes met, which happened whenever she passed by. It seemed he spent a lot of the time she was in his vision looking at her, an act that gave her the creeps even though she tried to think the best of him.

By lunchtime he had installed the panel and an alarm receptor in her kitchen. He took his break by excusing himself. She heard the front door shut and peered out the window, watching as he climbed back into the blue and white truck where he sat and ate alone.

She considered calling Alex but knew that would put her in a place that would make her sound paranoid. She was sure Alex was aware Damian worked for BTA. Calling him would make her look incapable and fearful, two things she fought vehemently against.

No, she would go on about cleaning and simply ignore the man.

She scrubbed the tub on her hands and knees, and heard movement that was not her own. Her heart pounding, she jerked around. He stood in the doorway holding his steel case. From the look on his face he was enjoying the view of her backside.

"I'm done in the living room and kitchen," he told her. "I was going to do the bathroom next but since you're in here I'll go on to the bedrooms. They back this way?" he tilted his head toward the hall.

She scurried up, brushing the hair out of her face. "Yes, they are."

"Three?" he asked.

"Yes," she nodded, absently squeezing the sponge in her hand dripping bleach-ridden cleanser down her jeans.

"You're…" he nodded his head toward her then, and made a move to come into the bathroom as if to help her. It was embarrassing the way her body jerked when he did, the way her hands flew out to stop him. Awkward silence filled the tiny space, as the memory of a night long ago swirled in the air between them.

"It's okay," she finally said. "I can take care of it."

He nodded and stepped back into the doorway. He gave her another look, one that bore understanding of how she really felt about him, and that she indeed had not forgotten, nor forgiven that night before he turned and was gone. She heard his faint prattling and let out a sigh.

You idiot, she told herself then. Poor guy, he was only trying to help. Now look what you've done. She'd ruined a perfectly ratty pair of jeans with bleach drips.

About to go change, she remembered that Damian was in one of the bedrooms too late, and found him in hers, right at her window. She stopped in the door, thinking better of it. She could wait until he was in Rebekah's room to change.

He was positioning the small plastic receiver on the frame of the window, just under the lock when she came in, and he turned. Her bedroom usually smelled of her perfume, her fabric softener on freshly washed sheets. The cigarette he must have smoked at lunch hung invisibly in the air. It was hard for her not to be taken by the smile that curled his lips. His eyes flicked to her bed and back to her.

"You need something?" he asked.

"Uh, no. I was going to change, but I'll wait until you're done."

He pulled the electric screwdriver out of his tool belt and flicked it on. But his eyes stayed on hers. "I can wait out in the hall."

"No. That's okay." Even the idea of having him in the

hall, just a locked door between them, gave her the creeps.

She backed out of the room nervous as a cornered cat. Reaching for her cell phone, again she debated calling Alex, but she'd already told herself why that was a bad idea. Times like this had her wishing her older brother lived near by. Times like this even had her wishing she *had* a man in her life – one that could just be a presence when a presence was necessary.

Scolding herself for even wanting to lean on someone left her in a foul mood. When a knock came at her door, she grumbled over, pulling it open with all the fury of a woman utterly frustrated.

Alex's handsome face drained that fury instantaneously.

"Hey." He wore sable slacks and another beautiful, silky black shirt with long sleeves, alluringly open to the middle of his chest. He must have hundreds of them, she thought with admiration, because he looks absolutely fabulous in them. "I came by to see how the alarm was coming along. I see they're still here." He gestured to the truck in her driveway with a tilt of his head.

"Yes, he's still here."

"Can I come in?"

"Yes, yes, of course." Her lungs filled with the balmy scent of him when he passed. Her eyes soaked up his profile, then swept him from head to toe. "You look very nice." She couldn't believe she'd said that. Compliments were not something she had planned on giving him anywhere – not even on the dance floor.

She could see she'd pleased him; his brown eyes sparkled. His gaze wandered her front, lingered on her bottom half at the bleached spots on her jeans. It was then that she remembered.

"What happened?" he asked.

"Cleaning." She shrugged on a fluttering laugh. Though she was far from comfortable around Alex, having him there was as settling as having a Doberman at her side.

"So," she started, smoothing her hair without thinking. "You must have been pretty surprised when you heard about Damian."

Any pleasure on his face vanished instantly at the mention of his high school friend. His dark brows creased. "What about him?"

"He's here."

Alex's eyes widened. "Here?"

"Yes, I thought you knew. He works for BTA. He's installing the system."

As if he'd been struck by a bolt of lightning, Alex's entire body grew taut. "He's here? In your house?"

Again she nodded, wondering at his reaction. "I figured you knew, arranging the job and all."

For the first time since she had opened the door, his eyes left hers and searched. "Where is he?"

"In the back." Without invitation or hesitation he walked briskly in that direction and she followed. When he stopped in her bedroom door, she saw him stiffen. She was safely behind him, but she wasn't sure why he seemed to have planned it that way. They both stood, her peering over his shoulder, looking at Damian.

Damian had just finished her second window and caught their movement in the door. He froze, staring back.

Lauren tried to read the silent messages passing between the two men. They faced each other like fighters in opposite corners of the ring.

Finally, Damian's hands fell casually to his side, and he

smiled. "Well, if it isn't Alex Saunders. How you doing, man?" He came toward them, his eyes taking in every detail of the way Alex stood, protectively blocking her.

Lauren watched Damian purposefully graze the corner of her bed with his thigh, as he came over with his hand out and ready to shake Alex's. The move apparently didn't go unnoticed by Alex because he stood more erect.

Alex shook his hand, but it didn't linger with the natural joy of reunion. "What are you doing here?"

Damian lifted his shoulders, keeping the casual grin on his face. "Installing this lovely lady's alarm." He pointed to the two of them. "Are you two a couple?"

Lauren wasn't about to let Damian or Alex get the wrong idea. "No," she piped, bringing Alex's gaze sideways down to her. "Just friends."

Damian let out a laugh that caused Alex to shift in the door. "Now that's something I never thought I'd see. How did you swing that one, bro?"

"Perhaps a more mystifying question would be how you got in the security business? Didn't you do jail time, *bro*?"

Damian's face shifted to stone. He glanced at Lauren, as if gauging her reaction to the news. Her eyes widened. "That was years ago, you know that." In an effort to redeem himself, Damian spoke quickly but with obvious effort to control the anger in his voice. "My record's clean now."

"So clean that you're installing security systems?" Alex leaned in the door, crossing his arms.

"So clean you could wipe your rich ass with it." Not to be intimidated, Damian picked up his steel briefcase and plowed by Alex, pausing when they were nose-to-nose. Lauren held her breath as male heat shocked the air.

"I'll believe it when I see it with my own eyes," Alex hissed between teeth.

"Be my guest." Damian twisted his head emphasizing the words. "It's down at the courthouse. Hell, maybe it's even online." He continued through the door without another word, straight into the other bedroom.

Alex moved to take off after him, but Lauren grabbed a hunk of his silk sleeve. It brought his hard-angled face right to hers. "What's going on?" she asked.

She'd seen him angry plenty of times – at her – but this fury surpassed anything she had witnessed before. The skin on his face had drawn tight over his cheekbones, around his eyes. His lips, usually full with inviting sensuality, were bitten back in a hard chord across his face. His body was ready to pounce as he loomed over her there in the hallway. She shirked back involuntarily, her heart pounding.

"I don't trust him," Alex's voice was purposefully low; she could tell he was trying to control it.

She swallowed a knot of fear. "But, he's your friend."

"He hasn't been my friend since—"He stopped, eyes skimming her face. Concern flashed in their depths then, and she placed her hand over her pounding heart. "We haven't been friends for years," he finished.

"Oh."

"I can't believe you let him in your house."

"What was I supposed to do? He's the installer."

"He's got a criminal record, Lauren. Damn it." Now he paced the tight space, and she shrunk against the wall, the storm of him frightening.

"I didn't know," she offered, but he just shot her a glare. That glare was enough to ignite her speck of a fuse. "Hey, it's not my fault. You're the one that insisted on the alarm system. If you hadn't—"

"Don't give me that." He was in her face again, and her back went flat against the wall. "You needed it. You'd have gotten it on your own."

"True," she shot back. "But maybe I'd have called another company."

He pounded one hand on the wall just over her head, sending a jolt through her. Tempted as she was to dart out of the hall into the safety of somewhere – anywhere, she doubted she could get by him. He leaned over her, practically closing her in, and the fury emanating from him was like the resonating vibes of a bear at full roar bouncing off the walls around them.

Her knees shook, her hands trembled, but she tilted her chin his direction. "I don't know why you're getting so riled about this," she said. "I've talked with him. He seems to be…to be…" she wouldn't tell him she'd been nervous the entire time Damian had been there. Or that her stomach had an ache in it now, what with the criminal news. "He seems to be changed."

Alex snorted. "Yeah, right." His hand was still anchored just above her head, as if he might at any moment wrap it around her throat in an effort to choke some sense into her. "You didn't know him like I did. It's obvious that you have no idea what your little security installer has been up to since we all partied in high school."

"*We* didn't party," she snapped, and it brought her body away from the wall and closer to his. Her breasts brushed his chest, her nose was just at his lips. "*You* partied, Alex. It was you and your band of hormonally-challenged friends that pounced on me that night in the parking lot."

His hand slid slowly down the wall and the heat of it warmed her ear, shot a buzz down her neck. She thought he was going to pull back and add the space they so desperately needed, but he only lifted his other hand and caged her in.

The fierceness in his eyes slowly changed to a very different fury now, one that encompassed Damian and the horrendously frightening night so long ago, but something more. Alex pulled himself upright, standing at his full height, reminding her of everything that he was: strong, male and indomitable. If he meant to make her feel incapable of taking him on, he was doing a good job of it.

Her knees nearly buckled, but more mortifying was the quivering sensation running loose inside of her like a mouse teasing, tempting, waiting to be caught. She drew her lower lip through her teeth, wondering why she enjoyed that he made her feel such delicious things when she should slap his smug face.

Instead, she worked to control her breath, now tattered as it came in and out. Her heart beat fitfully against her ribs. His eyes grew dark, sending her body into a tight fist begging to be opened.

Disgusted with her thoughts and feelings, she turned her head, closed her eyes. It was despicable that she wanted him so – that she responded to his methods with the ease of a virginal schoolgirl yearning for her first caress.

Even with Damian just a few feet away, Alex could dissolve into her right there in the hall. What's gotten into you, he wondered, studying her profile now that she had turned her face away. A sliver of satisfaction cut through him. He'd broken her, and he'd meant to – with a nice reminder that he was a man, and she was a woman.

Pressuring her into submission heated him to the core, and now he wanted to take her face in his hands and smother her with his kiss.

Get a hold of yourself, man. Electric as this moment was, as sizzling as he knew it could get, they still had a third party just beyond the threshold across the hall.

When he thought of Damian being in the same room with her, he wanted to kill him. He'd made a silent vow that night Damian had almost lost control – that she would never be anywhere near that man again.

Alex had not known how he would follow through with that promise; he and Lauren hadn't exactly been on speaking terms after that. But he'd known that if the opportunity ever came, he'd make sure she would never have to face Damian again.

And he'd failed.

His own effort to help her backfired, and she'd been alone with the man for who knows how long. Thankfully he'd gotten there when he had.

To look at her now, her face turned as if she were close to tears, stole every punch of desire he'd just felt. He wanted to take her against him, hold her, stroke her hair, then kiss her, but not with the heated passion that had just surged through his system rather with relief that she was safe.

He ran a finger along the exposed tendon of her neck, and she started. Did he frighten her that much? The thought shamed him, and he drew back, taking in a ragged breath lowering his head for a moment.

When he finally had the nerve to look at her, her blue eyes still held fear, but also gut-wrenching caution that told him he'd stepped over the line and blown it big time. It would be a long road in rebuilding what few, smooth stones they had laid between them.

Sufficiently leveled by the look on her face, he was ready to apologize when they both heard Damian clear his throat.

sixteen

Alex wasn't sure how much Damian had seen. Gauging by the fact that his briefcase still swung a bit in his hand, he figured Damian had just come through the door and probably had not been witness to his brainless behavior.

"I've finished in there," Damian said.

It was her opportunity to slip away from him and Alex didn't stop Lauren, not with Damian grinning across the hall. But he wasn't happy about it. He wanted to apologize.

Lauren started for the living room. "Thank you, Damian."

"I'll hit the bathroom and then I'll take you through the procedure to set up your password."

"That would be great, thanks."

Alex decided he would get to that apology just as soon as he finished grilling his old pal. Once Damian slid into the bathroom, Alex planted himself in the door. "Who in their right mind would give an ex-con a job installing security systems?"

Damian tugged his cordless screwdriver out of his tool belt. "Somebody with the brains to dig deep enough to find that people – even people with records – can change." He positioned the plastic receiver on the window frame and began drilling.

Alex shook his head with a snort of disagreement, but inside he wondered if it was possible. Maybe Lauren was right, maybe Damian had left his past behind. He certainly looked the trustworthy part. But Alex knew the guy had been vain enough to stow a mirror in his back pocket.

Rehabilitated or not, Alex wasn't about to leave it to chance. He'd give the guy the benefit of the doubt, but keep a close eye on things where Lauren was concerned. "So I heard you were trying to get in touch with me," he said.

Damian held the receiver in one hand, the screwdriver in the other, the tool buzzing. "Yeah, I was. Had a nice talk with your mom. She told me how your dad was." He looked over then, watched for Alex's reaction. Alex shifted in the doorway. "Still the same, huh?"

"You didn't look me up just to satisfy your curiosity about my father."

Damian's hands fell to his sides. "What's with you? We haven't seen each other in twelve years, and you're acting like what happened between us happened last night. What's your problem?"

Taking his shoulder away from the jamb, Alex stood upright, arms crossed. "I guess I'm a little skeptical. I mean, last time I saw you, you were straddling Lauren, ready to rip into her. Now you're setting up her security system."

"Hey, it was just as big of a surprise to me when she opened the door this morning."

"I'll bet."

"You think I planned this?" Screwdriver clenched in his fist, Damian crossed the small bath to his old friend. "Talk about issues." His dark eyes were hard. "You became your own worst nightmare after your pop's accident, Alex. Everything you hated about everybody else – spiteful, angry and distrusting."

Alex could feel his blood start to boil. Part of what his old friend said was true, but no one had ever had the nerve to say it to his face. For all that Damian was or had done, he'd once been Alex's closest friend, and Alex couldn't ignore that that had entitled him to a deeper look.

They stared at each other for a few minutes, neither saying anything. Alex could hear Lauren moving around somewhere in the house, and thinking of her softened the hard edge of his pride.

"Maybe I'm wrong," he kept his voice low so their conversation would not be overheard by Lauren. "If I am, time will tell me. I hope I am. Either way, stay away from her." He jerked his head Lauren's direction.

A smile hinted on Damian's lips. "You've had it for her ever since I can remember."

Alex had to swallow. He stuck his hands in his front pockets. "We're friends."

Damian backed himself to the window and continued working, his smile spreading. "Hey, that's more than it was in high school. Can't say I blame you." Repositioning the screwdriver, he flicked it on. "She's hot."

"Stay away from her."

"Why so protective if she doesn't belong to you?"

"She does belong to me." Alex was near to hissing. "I watch out for her. That's why you're here, installing this system. She's my responsibility."

"Simmer down, old buddy." Damian's laugh was just as low, just as sharp as Alex's hiss. "She's a grown woman. She can make choices for herself."

He was close to grabbing Damian by the shirt and throwing him against the tile wall but forced control. "She's not on the market. And if she were, you're the last person she'd want."

Having installed the receptor, Damian stuffed the tool in his belt with a smile and a shrug. The smugness was all it took. Alex took a step inside the bathroom with a snarl.

"What's going on?" Lauren asked from the door.

The two men froze.

"Just catching up." Damian's cordial smile and cold eyes slid back to Alex. "Weren't we, buddy?" He patted Alex's shoulder before passing him. Picking up his steel case he purposefully brushed Lauren's body with his as he went through the doorway.

He disappeared then, and Lauren turned her confused gaze to Alex. "What was that all about?"

He was next to her, looking down into her face. "I want to talk to you."

She peered down the hall where Damian had just vanished into the living room. "And I want to talk to you." She poked his chest with her finger. "What was that all about, 'she belongs to me, she's my responsibility'?" Her eyes were on fire. "I can't believe you'd stand there and tell him—"

"The truth," he said between teeth, leaning close. "The truth is you are my responsibility now. Everything you do concerns me because it concerns you and how you will perform."

Her eyes widened, her mouth fell open. Alex knew things were close to spiraling out of his control. "Look." He reached out to put calming hands on her shoulders but she batted him away.

"Don't touch me," she snapped. "I am not your property. I may be an investment, but that does not give you the right to control my life."

He might as well have dug himself a pit. He was ready to

throw his hands up in the air. "Lauren, this is not—"

"You're damned right it's not. There is nothing between us but your sponsorship got it?"

"Uh, are we ready?" Damian looked at them from the end of the hall.

"Very," Lauren growled and strode down the hall to him.

Not to be undermined by anyone, not even the woman he cared about who couldn't care less about him, Alex followed, amazed at the beating his ego was willing to take when it came to Lauren.

Alex stood in the background as Damian carefully explained how the system worked, taking her through the steps of setting up her password. Even trying to give Damian the benefit of the doubt, he didn't like that she was being so pleasant to him, and he was especially uncomfortable when Damian asked her for her password so he could show her how to arm and disarm the unit.

"You can change the password anytime," Damian added.

After Damian watched her go through all of the steps he shook her hand with a smile Alex thought could have fooled the devil.

"It was great seeing you, Lauren," Damian said. "What a coincidence, huh?"

"Yes, it was."

"If you have any problems at all with the system, here's my card." He reached into his shirt pocket with two fingers and brought out a card. "Call me anytime."

That was when Alex took his chances and moved closer to Lauren's side. He fought to keep his hands casually in his front pockets when they were itching to open the front door and push the guy out.

Damian looked at him, stuck out a hand. "Good to see you, buddy."

"Yeah." Alex's shake was brief.

Damian handed him a card as well. "Call me. We can go get a drink sometime. Wait—" Damian grinned. "I don't drink anymore." His grin slid to Lauren. "But there are a lot of other things to do."

Alex's eyes narrowed. He reached over and opened Lauren's front door, heard the chime signaling the door was open.

"Anytime a door or window opens, that chime will go off, unless it's on silent mode," Damian commented. Noting Alex's anxious posture, Damian slowed his advance to the front door. "I just need you to sign here, Lauren." He whipped out a clipboard with some paperwork and a pen on it. Lauren scrawled her name across the bottom line and handed it back to him.

"You have a thirty-day money back guarantee," Damian went on. Alex was sure he was dragging out the moment just to annoy him. "If at any time you have difficulties with the system there will be no cost to you," he turned to Alex with one corner of his lip curled, "or Alex."

Alex cleared his throat and dipped his head for a moment. Lauren thanked Damian again before he left. She shut the door, listening to the soft chime that would buy her some peace of mind, at least where Rebekah was concerned.

Some kind of strange male infighting had been going on between Alex and Damian. She didn't like that Alex had dragged her into it. She turned, her back pressed against the door, and leveled him a censuring glare. Then she waited for him to explain himself.

He shifted, squirmed even, and that pleased her. Rubbing the back of his neck, he looked at his fancy leather shoes.

"I guess I have to apologize," he said, still unable to meet her gaze.

"I guess you do."

"Okay." She felt a light tremor of satisfaction when his brown eyes met hers. "I'll admit I was wrong for being such an idiot in the hall. But I'm not sorry about anything else, Lauren. I don't know the guy anymore, and you never knew him at all. The point is, until I know I can trust him, I won't trust him. Not with you, not with anybody."

"That's between you and him. To me, he seemed perfectly fine, and I resent you dragging me into your personal battle."

He stepped her direction. "You were part of that battle, for your information," he snapped before realizing he'd incriminated himself.

She angled her head quizzically. "Surely you two weren't arguing over what happened in that parking lot. He apologized for that. It was the first thing he did when he walked through my door."

Alex took the step back that he'd taken, surprised by the news. "He did?"

"Then you come in here and pounce on him. It makes you look like a—"

"I know what it makes me look like." He was getting angry again, his pride taking another hit. He didn't like that she suddenly felt like sand vanishing through his fingers. "Do we have to talk about this?"

"Because it's uncomfortable for you, you want to go

around it. That's not the way I handle things, Alex."

"I don't go around anything, babe. You want to talk about it? Fine, let's talk."

"Start by telling me why you freaked when you found out he was here, and it's not just because he spent the night in jail."

"He spent more than a night." Alex jammed his hands through his hair. It was obvious Lauren had no idea the extent of Damian's involvement with the law.

"Okay, so tell me, what did he do that landed him in jail?" she asked.

If she knew he'd been in for assault maybe she wouldn't be so ready to forget. "He was charged with a count of domestic violence against his wife. She said he raped her, but, of course they were never able prove it."

Her face whitened, her eyes went wide. Good, he thought, at least she's taking me seriously. "He spent six months in county for it."

"Oh." Her hand fluttered at her breastbone.

"Beat the heck out of her, too."

"And his daughter?"

"As far as I know he didn't touch her. How did you know about his daughter?"

"He, uh…we were just talking."

He was sorry now that he'd told her, now that she looked whitewashed. He moved closer, wanting to reach out. "I don't want you to get hurt."

Off in thought, Lauren didn't notice that he'd closed the space between them. Her crossed arms brushed his chest, the pupils of her eyes dilated with concern.

"Lauren," he spoke softly, ran a finger along her

shoulder. She looked up at him. "You're right, I have no claim on you. I can't stop you from choosing whomever you want to befriend, all I ask is that you be careful."

She nodded, her hand still absently patting her breast. She took in a deep breath, but he could see her mind whirling.

"Satisfied?" he asked, tracing her shoulder, down the length of her arm to her hand. Then he gently took her hand in his and lifted it to his chest. He liked that her eyes snapped to emerald.

"Not yet," she said, easing her hand free. "That wasn't the only reason. There's more."

No way would he tell her he couldn't stand any man, other than himself and maybe Chad, being alone with her. "What other reason would I have? I thought you might be in danger."

She considered him and his words for a moment. "Oh, I think there are plenty of other reasons, Alex. Why you don't just come right out and admit the reasons is the mystery."

He felt the first twist of panic that she might know the breadth and depth of his feelings for her, feelings growing even with his pristine efforts to control them.

"What are you talking about?" he asked.

She headed to the front window, looked out as if expecting something or someone, and his heart plunged thinking it might be the boyfriend she'd alluded to. "As long as we're straight on our relationship." She looked at him over her shoulder. "That it's strictly professional."

For now, he thought, crossing to join her at the window. "Expecting someone?"

"Yes." She looked up at him with a smile that taunted, and it set him on edge. "I am, as a matter of fact."

She was satisfied, now that she had regained her place in the game. He'd tried to knock her down earlier with that power play in the hall. She'd almost left herself open for whatever he'd been prepared to do to her. Even recalling it sent a trickle of pleasure through her system. She didn't care if she and Alex sparred, she could deliver punches just as long as he could.

He was jealous, that was what he was hiding. It amused her, but it certainly didn't surprise her, not with their past. It still baffled her. Why he would be jealous of a woman with no material wealth, a handicapped child and a dead single life was a conundrum she wondered if she would ever understand.

Whatever his reasons, she owed him. She had the alarm now, and she was grateful for that.

There were days when she couldn't wait to see her child's little face peering out the window of the bus as it pulled up in front of the house. Today the pleasure would be double, knowing Alex was tied in knots thinking that she was waiting for some handsome hunk to pull into her driveway.

She snuck a glance at his profile, hard-lined and intense as he searched out the window for the unknown. It was cruel of her to mislead him. But she wasn't going to lose sleep over it. He deserved it after what he'd done today. He'd been a real jerk. Her mother always said, "Nothing cures ills like the taste of your own medicine." Lauren couldn't agree more. She only wished she could play up the moment but there wasn't enough time for anything fun like that. She felt sure other opportunities would arise and she would continue to push his buttons just like he pushed hers.

The rumble of a diesel engine told her the bus was barreling up the street. When the big yellow beast came to a stop in front of the house, she glanced at Alex and almost broke out into laughter, he looked so relieved.

Instead, she greeted the driver through the open bus door and waited with her arms out for Rebekah.

seventeen

Though Rebekah was a good thirty pounds, Lauren carried her like an infant on her cocked hip. "How was school today?" She asked questions as if she expected a normal conversation to ensue. Lauren believed that somehow, the information was registering in some far-off place in Rebekah's brain and that someday, when pathways were sufficiently mended, there would be conversation. It was a long shot, but it was better than the alternative of hopelessness.

"Did you work hard for your teacher? Did you eat all of your lunch?"

Inside, she found Alex waiting. She half expected him to look awkward, the usual response of someone unfamiliar with dealing with individuals who had disabilities. He looked remarkably relaxed, anticipating, even. She decided not to continue her game of teasing him for the time being.

"Rebekah, this is Alex."

"Hello, Rebekah."

"Do you remember Alex? He was here the other night. Remember the night you ran?"

Rebekah spared Alex a fleeting glance and wriggled out of her mother's arms. Her eyes instantly lit on the new alarm pad right by the front door. It amazed Lauren that her child could seem so unaware one moment and totally focused the next.

"That's our new alarm." Lauren showed her the buttons, how it made a little chime when she opened the door. Rebekah's blue eyes were wide with wonder as she babbled.

"Alarm," Lauren said and repeated until Rebekah finally garbled the word. "Yes, that's right." She squeezed her tight. "Now Mommy will know when the door opens and you will be safe, little angel." She kissed her, and swung her into place on her hip again, then looked at Alex.

Was it possible that his heart could take another squeeze? It had, the moment Lauren's face lit at the sight of that bus. This squeeze was different than the one he'd felt when he'd learned that Damian was in her house. Something unspeakably beautiful had come over her, something he'd seen reflected in his own mother's face when she'd been looking at those photos of him. But not only then, Alex realized he'd been witness to that very look countless times throughout his life from people that loved him. It was humbling.

Mothers were blessed with a gift he doubted he would ever be able to duplicate, yet he knew then he wanted to very much. Part of it stemmed from having his father taken from him at an early age. Then there was this new feeling he carried inside for Lauren, appreciation for what she endured each and every day, without any reciprocation from her child, and yet it didn't stop her from loving.

It tore his heart.

Rebekah hummed and babbled, squirmed and whined, and he found himself unable to take his eyes from the scene. The little girl looked so normal, if he hadn't known that she had autism, he'd have thought she was just a regular kid.

"She doesn't look—" he'd spoken his thoughts before he'd had a chance to edit them for political correctness and he shoved his hands in his pockets, dropping his head for a moment.

"That actually makes it harder – especially in public."

Lauren eased Rebekah down, took her hand and led her into the kitchen. "If she looked obviously handicapped, people might be a little more understanding. And forgiving."

Alex followed her into the kitchen and watched Rebekah sit at the kitchen table.

"It's hardest when children are waiting in line for something, like at a park. Or when we're waiting for food at McDonald's or some place like that. Rebekah doesn't get the whole wait-your-turn-thing, so she just bowls through the line and that upsets a lot of kids, not to mention their parents." Lauren looked at Rebekah who sat tapping the table with a key chain Alex had not even seen her find.

"Rebekah, what do you want to eat? Use your words and tell Mommy."

"Orange."

"Very good using your words." Lauren dug an orange out of the refrigerator, set out the cutting board and began slicing off the skin. "It took over a year of work with a speech therapist for me to be able to get her to verbalize with even one word." She sliced the orange into bite-size pieces. "My goal is to get her using three-to-five word sentences."

Placing the plate in front of Rebekah, Lauren said, "Thank you, Mommy."

Although Rebekah didn't repeat the words, nor did she look Lauren in the eye, she made a grunting of syllables.

"Wow." Alex was completely flabbergasted at the effort it took to communicate with the child. The never ending, tireless work of mother, teacher and specialist that he now understood went into bringing children like this out of their shells.

"She seems happy," he commented, noting her disposition was cheerful. She smiled and giggled, even if it was at things no one could see.

"Oh, she's very happy." Lauren gently patted her head, and Rebekah looked at her briefly. "I'm lucky that way. So many children with autism are locked in these little bodies and they just seem tormented, you can see it on their faces."

"No kidding."

"And she's not as sensitive to touch as a lot of children." Lauren's hand lingered with caution on Rebekah's head, then her fingers traced the soft, pale skin of her neck. Rebekah scrunched her head and started giggling. Alex couldn't imagine how hard it would be to want to touch a child and be unable. In his mind, children were meant to be held and loved.

"That must be hard," he murmured.

Lauren studied the ponderous look on his face. "It can be. There have been times I've held her against me, just needing the contact so badly, and she's fought me." Her gaze returned to her daughter, her fingers again trailing her head and neck, and again Rebekah broke out into giggles, this time followed by a screech.

"Her brain doesn't work fast enough for her to say, *stop it*. So she'll just make a noise like that. But, hey, at least she's tying an appropriate response to an action. That's something."

He was staggered, Lauren could tell. She'd dealt with enough people to know when words couldn't express the depth of their shock over what it was like to live with a child like hers.

Lauren had no idea what this raw revelation would do to her relationship with Alex and for a moment felt a grain of dismay. "I'm so accustomed to it, I sometimes forget how it looks to others," she lied. She never forgot, and found the quivering of wonder in her nerves surprising while she waited for Alex to say something.

His dark gaze stayed fixed on Rebekah's every move. "It looks like a sacrifice of unspeakable magnitude." The gentle caring in his voice made Lauren's heart skip.

Though things between them were far from peachy, she wouldn't lie to herself and pretend that she didn't enjoy their playful bantering, even volatile as it could get. She would miss it if he chose to move on.

But her child came before anything she might enjoy or want. Lauren didn't keep opportunity at arm's length to be masochistic in anyway. She could enjoy a new friendship, an opportunity, just like anyone else. But when it came down to it, she was all that Rebekah had. Most men went running when the pumpkin broke apart and they didn't care for what was inside.

Rebekah finished her orange and got up to get another. Lauren held the refrigerator door shut, looking at her. "Look at mommy, please."

Pulling on the refrigerator handle, Rebekah squealed and squeaked, but did not look at Lauren in her attempt to retrieve another orange.

"Look at Mommy, Rebekah, and tell me what you want. Use your words."

Still striving with all of her might to open the door Rebekah finally squeaked, "Orng."

"Excellent using your words and asking. Go sit down and mommy will cut another orange." Lauren half wondered why Alex was still there. Hadn't he seen enough? He seemed amazingly at ease, curious even. Maybe, like a lot of people, he'd seen so few individuals with autism he was simply fascinated and wanted to watch. In Lauren's book, there was only one place she liked being observed, and that was on the dance floor.

"So." She diced the orange and placed it in front of Rebekah who immediately dug in with her fork. Lauren looked at Alex. "Seen enough?"

He'd been deep in thought; she could tell by the way he kind of started, looking from Rebekah to her. "Oh. What?"

A man his age should know better than to stare, she thought, and put herself in the line of his vision. "Done?"

Something had ticked her off, and Alex wasn't sure what it was. But he had the distinct impression it had to do with him. "Done?" he queried.

"Listen, thanks for the alarm." She looked at him without covering her smirk. "It's going to be great." Then she started for the front door, but he didn't follow her. He was too entranced with Rebekah.

She didn't look much like her mother, Alex decided. Her mousy blonde hair fell in tangles to her back, softly fringed around her cherubic face. And she had the most incredible blue eyes – big and round as the Dutch plates hanging on the wall. Lauren had been right to call her 'little angel'; the child looked freshly plucked from heaven.

More than her angelic beauty, Alex was completely taken by the way she existed as if nothing around her mattered, and yet the whole of her surroundings impacted her. She couldn't stop looking – at the walls, the ceiling, a crumb on the table, out the window, at her mother, at him. As if she couldn't take it all in fast enough.

What was all of it doing in her head, he wondered and drew up a chair, sitting at the table with her. She looked at him then, and Alex felt what he imagined Lauren felt – a small thrill that she had granted him her attention for even a second.

He found the little noises she made sweet and endearing. Chirps, hums, grunts and tunes, all with the soft, warbled voice of an angel just learning to sing.

Her hands were deft, her delicate fingers in motion with the constancy of shallow water over stones. Always, her gaze flew about the room. When and if it met his, he felt an incredible surge he'd only felt one other place in his life – when his father had looked at him, after the accident.

They were much the same, Alex decided then. Both trapped in bodies that wouldn't respond the way they wanted them to. He was sure both his father and Rebekah were at a point where neither really knew what their bodies were capable of. At least he hoped that. It was too cruel and unfair to think of the other alternative.

"Is that good, Rebekah?" he asked. She was swinging her legs under the table, now singing a little cross of notes without melody or reason other than that she liked making the noises with her voice.

"I like oranges too," he said. "My mommy used to cut them up just like that for me when I ate them."

Rebekah had focused on something overhead and Alex followed her gaze to the ceiling but saw nothing. "What do you see?" he asked. "Do you see something?"

Suddenly, she was looking at him and his heart gave a little start. A flash of emotion welled behind his eyes. He wanted more than anything for her to speak to him, to say something. To know what she was thinking. Finished with her orange, she left the table and, babbling, vanished around the corner.

Alex watched her, amazed and not surprisingly

saddened. She lived in her own world, a place she was clearly at home in. A place others were only invited to when she granted it, however brief the invitation, however fleeting the moment. Even then, you would never really be there with her for she occupied the whole of it completely, without the need or desire for companionship. His gaze finally wandered, and came to rest on Lauren, standing with her arms crossed.

He stood. His heart opened and he felt straining fingers of compassion for her. The urge to hold her grew stronger with each step. Looking down into her eyes, he wanted to help.

The alarm system was not going to be enough.

"She's beautiful," he murmured.

Surprise flickered in her eyes. For a moment, she struggled with what to say, and he liked that. "Thank you."

"Tell me more about her."

"Excuse me?"

"Does she always look around like that? Like she's trying to see everything all at once?"

"It's called visual stimming," Lauren told him, surprised by his sincere interest. "Stimming?"

"Children with autism constantly self stimulate in one way or another. It's one of the main reasons they have a barrier to learning. They can't stop themselves."

"Interesting. I'd heard about autistic children flapping, but I didn't know—"

"They're not autistic." Nothing drove her battier than the blanket term. "They *have* autism. The child *isn't* autism." She knew her voice was rising, but she didn't care. "It's not who she is or what she is. She's still a little girl. She still likes oranges, and swinging, and climbing the monkey bars. She likes baths and soap bubbles and she likes to run." Furious tears filled her eyes.

Alex reached out and put his hands on her shoulders. "I'm sorry. You're right. That was insensitive of me."

"No. No, I'm sorry." She rubbed at her forehead on a sigh, and blinked the tears away. "It shouldn't bother me." Lauren crossed the living room and fell onto one of her couches. "After all this time, you'd think I'd have the skin of a rhinoceros, but I don't. I can't stand it when people box children with handicaps, limiting them, taking away the fragile possibilities of their future – as if they don't have enough injustice. It drives me crazy when I hear someone say, '*Oh, he's a down's.*' He's not a down's; he's still an individual, created separately and uniquely, just like the rest of us. He happens to have Down's syndrome along with all of his other gifts and qualities."

It was then that Alex knew he loved her. Like a brick to his chest it hit him, hard and without any give. He couldn't run away from it. He couldn't toss the respect and admiration flowing inside for her out. It was as basic as his blood that he knew he would gladly give for her or her child.

He stood looking down at her, emotion rushing into his eyes. The image of her blurred. He hadn't allowed tears in so long he felt his cheeks color and looked away. Lauren sat forward, alarmed.

"Are you okay?"

He nodded and let out a self-depreciating laugh, sitting next to her on the couch. "It's just—" He looked at her then, not caring if he looked ridiculous, risking whatever she might think of a man who wore emotion on his cuff.

But the soft alarm in her face had vanished, and she wore the unmistakable look of scorn. "Look, don't feel sorry for me," her tone was hard. "I'm not some poor woman who's been dealt a lame hand you can pity."

"That's not it, Lauren. You're wrong."

She sat erect, clutching one of the throw pillows to her breast like she might tear it apart. Or use it to shield her heart. "I've seen it all, Alex. There is not one reaction that I haven't had thrown at me."

He didn't like that she'd accused him of something he was innocent of. He wanted to shake her, get her to loosen up, to open her eyes to an honest man eager to help. Most definitely, he did not want her to lump him in with all of the other losers that had obviously hurt her with their callousness.

More than that, he wanted to hold her against him. If he could convince her that he wanted to help her, shelter her, protect her, then maybe she would stay off the ferocious wagon she seemed to tear through life on just long enough to trust someone again.

He bet she'd not had every reaction thrown at her, and just to prove it, he reached out and snagged her, his arms wrapping around her waist. He pulled her across his lap so that she was looking up into his face as she lay in his arms.

Her eyes were wild with wonder and it shifted his bubbling frustration to desire. Her lips parted, ready to protest. Staring at them, he wanted her to feel the burn of his gaze before he'd even touched his mouth to hers.

Lowering his face, he felt her struggle, but he just tightened his grip. If she really wanted to be free, she could be. The struggle was just weak enough that he knew she wanted this as much as he did.

He covered her mouth with his, the taste of her shooting hot fire from their joined lips straight to his fingers and toes.

How long had he dreamt of this? Images flashed behind his eyes as repressed hunger took over. Since he'd first seen her, delectable curves budding into woman. That had been the beginning of his craving. He'd only been a boy, her teasing nothing compared to the voracious appetite that had grown cavernous after that night.

His had been a tortuous game, self-inflicted, as he'd followed her around like a pup anxious for a scrap, knowing full well a scrap wouldn't be enough. To feel the heat of her body under his now, to taste her lips and breathe her in as he devoured, spun his body into an insatiable need he knew in seconds would implode.

Responding to that need, his hands moved of their own accord, though he had the fleeting worry that by loosening his grip, she might flee. Searching fingers took in every muscle of her back, the long, elegant groove of her spine, the firm cut of her waist. One hand thrust into her hair at the base of her head, the desire to pull her into him so strong, his palm clutched, held her head still so that her lips were flush with his.

When her arms slid up and wrapped around him, another burst of fire trembled through him. She wanted him, just as much as he wanted her. Her body was falling more deeply into the soft seams of the couch encouraging him to cover her completely.

She stretched out underneath him, and he slid over, their lengths perfectly aligned. Male and female. The very hint of the position that could swallow them both had him deepening the kiss. Impatient hands drove into her hair, fisting, controlling the movement their mouths made together. Unable to get enough of her fast enough, he angled her head to comply with his demands.

Ready to tear into her, Alex shifted, positioning himself for a grander feast. But the sudden chime of the alarm had them both freezing.

Dazed, blood still at a high-pitched thrum, Alex kept his mouth hovering over hers, ready, needing more.

"Rebekah," her breathless whisper would have been exciting to him, had she not uttered her child's name, reminding him that the little girl could be in danger. He pulled himself up and marveled that she was out from under him and darting down the hall before he could sit up completely.

He heard her voice from Rebekah's bedroom. "No, Rebekah. No. You can't go out the window, angel." The girl's soft mumbling followed, and he straightened every tight fiber and stood, still coiled with suspended desire.

He was at Rebekah's bedroom door as quickly as a body rammed with need could get itself. His desire drained when he saw how she had shifted from hot and wanting, to mothering bird in a few seconds.

She looked up at him. "She was trying for the window." Standing, she kept Rebekah hoisted on her hip. He'd been sure the installation of the alarm would ease the troubling tension he'd seen on her face since that day Rebekah had run. As he crossed to her, he eyed the little girl staring about, whose faint hum sounded like it belonged to an infant rather than a child of five. She had no idea how all of this was affecting her mother. He ran a hand quickly atop her head. "You want to go out that window, don't you, baby?"

Rebekah looked at him for a minute before leaning toward the window with an affirmative grunt. And he wondered what possessed her, drove her to such obsession? Did she want to feel the cold night air? Perhaps it was as simple as the need for freedom, locked up as she was in a body that somehow, must know its limitations and yearn for more.

"What about nailing it shut?" When Lauren's expression flashed with disbelief, he said, "I know it sounds extreme." But in his mind, it looked like she had no other options. "That way, at least when you two go down for the night, you can rest. Think about it, what if you didn't hear the alarm for some reason? And even if you did, she could be halfway to who knows where by the time you got in here."

Indescribable guilt passed over Lauren's face and he ached inside, knowing what she was thinking. "But it sounds so…"

Gently he set a hand on her free shoulder. "I'm not going to pretend to know more about this situation than you do," he said softly. But he knew that desperation often drew from unorthodox reservoirs. His mother had sworn to never leave his father's side, when they slept, even in his disabled condition. In the end, the endless hums and belches of the machines, coupled with his father's labored wheeze had forced her back to her own bedroom at the other end of the house. She'd been eaten up with guilt about it for months.

"If there was an emergency, God forbid, you're one door away. She wouldn't be able to get out and be safe on her own, even if the window wasn't permanently shut."

Lauren's gaze was tight on Rebekah's distracted face. "You're right." She put Rebekah down, watched as she ran right back to the window, climbed up and worked the window latch again.

"No, no, Rebekah." In a second she had the wiggling child back in her arms, and was looking helplessly at Alex. Defeat hung in her countenance. He ran a hand down his face feeling part of her frustration.

"Where do you keep your tools?" he asked. He'd take care of the deed himself, he decided.

"In the garage, right by the steps – a red toolbox."

He was glad to be there with her now, helping her with this very domestic, if not undesirable chore. But at the same time, he wondered what kind of idiot leaves a woman like Lauren and an utterly defenseless child to take on the world alone? He knew then that if he ever came face to face with her ex, he'd debate slugging the man.

After retrieving the toolbox, he dug through it for a nail large enough to penetrate the casing and stay put.

One look at Lauren's face, wretchedly scored with guilt, and he thought he might as well have been installing chains and cuffs. She hated having to do this. Before he took his first swing at the nail, he asked, "Are you okay with this?"

"There's no other way, is there?"

"Not unless you want to sleep with her tied to you."

"She'd never sleep if I was in the room with her – I tried that before."

He set the hammer and nail aside and went to her, looked deep into her eyes and saw the shorn heart of a mother who would do anything for her child. "Lauren," he let out a sigh. "This is difficult, I know. I'd bet that hammer this isn't the first time you've had to make a decision like this – a decision based on reality, rather than common sense."

The line between her brows etched deep. "I know, and you're right. And for sure it's not the last time." There would be innumerable, Lauren was positive of that.

Alex gathered the hammer and nail and returned to the window. When she gave him one last nod to go ahead, he hammered the nail in place. Rebekah's eyes grew huge as she watched from her mother's hip. "Don't think about it in the conventional way," he added. "When a disability's involved, sometimes convention gets thrown out the window." He shrugged, grinned a little. "No pun intended."

She tried a laugh and crossed to look at his handy work.

"Chances are it won't be permanent," he went on, touching Rebekah's nose with his finger. She turned her head from him for a moment before turning back around to examine the nail.

"You're right." Lauren knew full well how Rebekah's fascinations fluctuated. Once she figured out the window was not going to open, she would move onto something else. Then she had a horrifying thought.

"Do you think I'll have to nail every window closed?" Despair set in as Lauren imagined never feeling a breeze cool a room again.

Rebekah wormed free of her mother's grasp and marched right back to the window and climbed, trying the window again.

"Do you think she'll try every one?" Alex asked.

"I don't know. The thing is, when she's home, usually Aubrey or I am with her. I guess we'll just have to see how it goes and take it from there." Lauren let out a sigh and reached for the toolbox, but Alex held it.

"I'll take care of it."

Lauren stared out the front window listening to Alex in the garage. The black shroud of evening had finally come, and with the commotion, she'd not even noticed. It wasn't cold, and she would have enjoyed cracking open the windows for the crisp, nightly air.

You're just feeling sorry for yourself. You have a state-of-the art security system and you're whining about a few closed windows. Pride kept her from wallowing any longer and when Alex came back in, she looked at him through the eyes of someone in debt.

He crossed to her, and the look of desire was back in his dark eyes. She felt an involuntary shudder slide down her back.

"I want to talk about what happened before she tried to open the window," his voice had the low hum of a motor just warming up.

No, he wasn't someone who avoided talking about anything. That was certain now. It was she who wasn't sure she wanted to talk about that kiss. It had zapped her strength, almost stolen her will. She'd glommed onto him with the fervor of someone who'd been fasting for three years and finally had the chance to eat.

"It was a mistake," she blurted, disappointed that she'd been so weak. So what if it had felt heavenly, consoling wrapped in his arms, covered by male strength. Too bad if his mouth had been a warm, soft magnet hers couldn't resist. She had told herself that she would never get involved with someone she was in a business relationship with and she'd gone back on her word.

His eyes sharpened. "A mistake? You're going to tell me you didn't enjoy it?"

"I didn't say that." Smoke slithered behind his eyes, and she inched back. "I said it was a mistake. Look, I don't get involved romantically with business partners. It's just not a smart thing to do."

"What if I disagree?"

"You have your right to, I guess. But I learned the hard

way to never mix business with pleasure. My ex was my dance partner and, I'm sorry, but that's just not an experience I can gloss over."

"And you shouldn't. But Lauren, not all men are like your ex." Since it appeared he inked into everything, Alex decided he would most certainly slug the man if he ever had the opportunity.

"What about your new man? Is it because of him?"

The very thought that he would never feel her heat against him, take her lips and anything more of her, shot frustration through Alex's system. He wouldn't settle for it. That would be like asking a bear to sit quietly on the banks of a river as a school of salmon swam by. Convincing her that she was utterly wrong would take time and finesse. And he knew now, love. Alex had abundance in all of those and she was well worth it. He figured his face must have shown his inner resignation, because the wariness brightening her green eyes vanished.

"That's fleeting." She turned, not wanting him to see the deception on her face. "Let me fix you some dinner," she said. It was the least thing she could do.

Snatching her elbow, he pulled her around. "How fleeting?"

He looked so earnest; she decided even if they could never have a relationship, she at least owed him honesty. "There is no man, or I wouldn't have kissed you like that, would I?"

Pondering her a moment, the pleasure in his eyes filled her insides. He released her elbow with the faintest curve in his lip. "I'm glad to hear that."

"I'm sure." She mirrored his smirk. "Now. Something to eat?"

He glanced at his watch. "We have some time before rehearsal at the studio, how about I take us out?"

"That's not necessary." She would only be stockpiling debt, however tempting a dinner out was. "I can put something together."

Heading into the kitchen, she tried to remember when the last time was that she had gone to the store. Out of necessity, she kept the special foods Rebekah could eat on hand. As for herself, she often scrounged.

"Come on, Lauren. You don't really feel like cooking, do you?"

How can he know that? she wondered, trying to disguise her amazement with a dipped head into the refrigerator. "I don't usually take Rebekah out," she told him. "She can act up sometimes, unexpectedly, be a handful."

Gently he pulled her up, his hands firmly holding her shoulders so that he could look her straight in the eye. A warm sensation much like the one she had felt when he'd had her pinned to the couch filled her, starting where his hands met her skin. "Tonight you've got an extra set of hands to help out."

eighteen

Eating out with Rebekah was as precarious as crossing a tight rope over a lava pit. Few dining establishments Lauren had researched offered any items that fit into her wheat-free, dairy-free diet. And it wasn't as simple as not eating items with wheat or dairy. Rebekah's sensitive system couldn't even tolerate food that had been prepared and thus contaminated in the same area with the offending foods. Involuntarily, she would become turbo-hyper, extra sensitive, and often angry, bordering violent, if she ingested the contaminated foods. It took days for her to come down from the high, leaving her dull and listless.

It was McDonalds they found themselves at, and Lauren caught herself glancing at the reflection of the three of them in the glass of the lobby. She found the sight pleasant.

After ordering, they sat in the playland and Rebekah joined the other half-dozen children monkeying all over the indoor play area with ball pit, two slides, climbing cages and soft Ronalds for punching.

Lauren kept an eye on Rebekah out her peripheral vision while she enjoyed a cheeseburger and Alex's company.

Eyeing Rebekah's food with interest Alex asked, "So you ordered her a plain burger with lettuce and pickles but no condiments and no bun."

"Because ketchup has corn syrup and that's a trigger food for her. She doesn't like mustard, though it's okay for her to eat."

"Wow." Alex bit into his Big Mac. "How did you learn all of this?"

"I went to an autism convention right after Rebekah was diagnosed, and the one thing that ninety percent of children with autism respond to, and that I could afford, was to change her diet."

"That's so intensive."

She nodded. "But worth it. See, milk peptides react just like opium peptides in the gut of a child with autism, producing the same reaction as an opium addict."

"No kidding." Alex followed Lauren's intense gaze to Rebekah, starting to climb the outside of the play land. Suddenly, Lauren darted over. Alex shot up and started over, then stopped. He was too far away to hear what mother was saying to daughter, but by the shake of Lauren's head, and the way Rebekah started to whine, he braced for the worst.

But Lauren only hoisted Rebekah onto her hip and carried her back with a smile. Setting her at the table with them, she said, "Eat your fries and burger, angel."

Obediently, Rebekah ate, twisting her body around so that her yearning eyes could take in the play set.

"The diet's a small price to pay." Lauren wiped one of Rebekah's greasy hands with a napkin, "to have even a little bit of my child back."

Alex could feel his stomach clutch. He knew first hand how difficult it was to deal with absolutes that could devastate and change the course of a life. In his case, he had known the man who had been his father well before tragedy had stolen him. What had Lauren known of Rebekah but a few short years? The torment that had ravaged him in his youth after his father's accident would be nothing compared to the what-if's and bleak hopelessness Lauren faced. And it would never be over, he thought, his gaze on Rebekah. She was eating lettuce leaves one at a time, just like any other child. Looking around, watching the children, staring up into nothingness. She was physically there but mentally somewhere else.

"So." He cleared thick emotion from his throat. He couldn't look at the innocent child, oblivious that her mere presence could stir him to tears. Her mother would be a safer subject. "Have you any prognosis for her?"

"It's not the same for every child. The projection is as vast as the umbrella under which the spectrum of the disorder reaches."

"I see."

"But I stay hopeful." Lauren reached out and ran a hand over Rebekah's head. "I'll do all that I can for her and hope it will be enough until something better comes along."

Desire to help had already burst inside that day he'd helped search for Rebekah. The feeling was insatiable now. "Is she getting all that she needs?"

"She's in a district program, and it's been good. I can't complain. At least it's something. But it's hardly adequate. Children with autism need constant intervention. High-impact programs really work best to pull them out of their comfort zones and into the world around them. I would love for her to be at Giant Steps."

"What's Giant Steps?"

"A private program specifically for children with autism. They do an eight hour a day applied behavioral program there. It's very intensive, but works wonders helping the children learn basic listening and learning skills necessary so that they can someday go on to more advanced academics."

"So why isn't she at Giant Steps?"

"They have a year-long waiting list."

Alex's brows synched as he sipped his Coke. "A year? There are that many children with autism?"

"One in one hundred and fifty, Alex."

Stunned, he looked at Rebekah, shoving the last bit of her meat into her eager mouth. Then she jumped off the chair and ran back to the play land and started to climb. As if she anticipated her mother's retribution, she looked over her shoulder at Lauren with a teasing giggle.

Clearly Lauren enjoyed the interaction – savored it, in fact. Though brief, it had been a very real silent communication. "She's teasing you," he commented.

"Oh, she's very smart." Lauren leaned both elbows on the table, her gaze dancing from her child to his. "She definitely knows how to manipulate and tease. It's amazing how she lacks something as basic as common sense and natural fear of danger, but understands just what buttons to push to get what she wants."

It was a conundrum he was fascinated by, and Alex continued to carefully watch Rebekah at play. The fine line between when she was tuned in to her surroundings and when she simply tuned out, staring off into nothing, fluttered.

"You're doing a great job with her," he finally said. If Lauren was his, he would have leaned over and kissed her then. The thought shot the blaze he'd felt earlier along every sinew and fiber inside. The want for her was growing out of control, his body taut with the need to make her his.

She was completely unaware, thankfully. He settled his want by just watching as she followed Rebekah's every move with those exotic green eyes.

He was ready to reach out and take her hands, hoping the small contact would pour water on the fire roaring through him, but he heard a familiar voice behind him and turned.

Nothing else could have effectively squelched desire like staring up into the devious eyes of his old friend.

"Well, well, well." Damian's smile slicked into place. "Twice in one day? This is a coincidence, isn't it?" His daughter, a bright-eyed seven year old with bouncing ponytails, tugged at his shirt.

"Daddy, can I go play?"

"Sure, baby." Damian's dark eyes shifted only momentarily to watch her go, then were right back on Lauren. He merely glanced at his old friend. "How's the system, Lauren? It's what," he glanced perfunctorily at his watch, "six hours old now? You got the hang of it?"

"It's fine, thanks."

Something inside of Alex pinched, disconcerted at the random sight of Damian. The chances of running into someone twice in the same day were slim to none; it was just too suspicious for his liking.

He stood. "Lauren, we'll be late if we don't head out now."

"Oh, you're right, I completely forgot about rehearsal. Let me get Rebekah. Nice to see you again, Damian."

"You too." Damian licked his lips like a wolf ready to take a bite, and Alex took it like a nail on bare skin.

Alex leaned toward him. "Of all the McDonald's in the county, you happen to choose this one?" He let out a sneer. "Stay away from her."

Damian's brows shot up in surprise. "I don't know what you're talking about, old buddy. I'm just taking my little girl out for a night of fun, just like—" he looked over Alex's shoulder at Lauren, smiled. "That's right, you two aren't a couple. I'm here as a single parent, just like Lauren."

Alex resisted the urge to grab Damian's black shirt in his fist. At that moment, he wished more than anything he could claim Lauren as his own and silence Damian for good.

"License to install her security system doesn't entitle you anything, *old buddy*."

"Did I hear her say something about a rehearsal? You still drooling around while she shakes that, mmm, luscious tail feather of hers? Although, I seem to remember it was her bunny tail that grabbed you by the balls."

Alex's fingers itched to snap around Damian's shirt. With the flick of a glance, Damian's brow cocked. "Looks like you've learned to control yourself."

Lauren's eyes were wide when she brought Rebekah over on her hip. Her gaze volleyed between the two men.

"Let's get out of here." Alex took her elbow and brought her close, his eyes burning into Damian's.

"Let me grab my purse."

Damian snapped it up with a glittering smile and handed it to her. "Here you go. Hey, you call me now if you have any trouble with the alarm. Promise?"

Confused by the tight vibe drawing the three of them together, Lauren nodded. "Sure. Thanks."

Lauren got Rebekah situated in her car seat, clipped her seat belt in place and got in the car.

The engine roared when Alex pressed on the accelerator, even though they were still in park. "He's an idiot." Backing out the car, his movements were jerky. His knuckles whitened on the steering wheel.

"He was eating dinner with his daughter," Lauren pointed out.

"You don't find it the least fluky that he was at the same place you were, after having spent the entire day in your house?" He shot her a glance from across the car, and her heart started to tap with concern.

"It's not that unusual, Alex. McDonalds is a pretty popular place."

"I don't like it."

"You think he's following me? That's ridiculous."

It's more than ridiculous, Alex steamed. He knew how smart his old friend was. You're insanely incredible, and any man would be blind not to want you for their own. He wanted to shout at her but bit back the urge with a laugh.

"You're probably right," he lied. If there were a bottom to it, he'd get to it.

Lauren put the pieces together. She had just kissed him not more than an hour ago. The sheer drive and power inside of him had lusciously pushed into her in a way that she had to respect as well as admire. He wanted her, and he didn't want anyone else to have her.

No wonder he had been angry when she'd told him how she felt about mixing business with pleasure. Smiling to herself, she enjoyed this secret knowledge. It merely confirmed her earlier thoughts, and gave her bone-trembling satisfaction.

Rebekah's mumblings eased the taut silence as they drove. Again, Lauren found herself considering the three of them, cozily driving together. To the casual driver passing by, they appeared to be a family out for an evening. It was a pleasant thought; one Lauren decided fit a niche in her heart that had been vacant so long, she was frighteningly close to embracing it.

She would have to be stronger against the draw of him,

tighten her resolve in spite of the fact that she could still feel his lips on hers. She glanced over. He sat with one hand on the wheel, the other tentatively rubbing his jaw, now darkening with a whispered shadow that was enticingly male. The sight of his strong profile had her stomach in a whirl.

Aubrey was waiting for them when they pulled up, and Lauren got out and unsnapped Rebekah's seat belt. "I'll just be a second," she told him.

He got out of the car without saying a word, and was at her side, ready to help her with Rebekah. The attentiveness impressed her.

Aubrey quickly ushered Rebekah inside with a shy smile and a dip of her head.

"Let me change and I'll follow you over." Lauren turned to head back to her bedroom, but Alex stopped her.

"I think I'll pass on rehearsal tonight."

He couldn't have surprised her more. Or disappointed her. She tilted her head at him. "You're not coming?" Whether she cared to admit it or not she rather enjoyed his charismatic presence in the studio, powerful and overshadowing as it was.

"I have some things I need to take care of." He reached out to touch her then withdrew, as if he thought better of it, and the little snip of disappointment in her heart was very real.

"Oh," she said. "Well, thank you again for the alarm system, Alex. It's a god-send."

"Change your password." It wasn't a reminder, but a request, and without a fight, she nodded.

Lauren watched him take the stairs down with an easy skip. She found herself wondering where he was going and just what he was going to do that was more important than watching her dance. Than hopelessly pining after her.

You're losing your head, she warned herself, wondering why the idea didn't bother her now like it used to. With a laugh, she went inside to change.

nineteen

Money had been Alex's only sibling – without a doubt more fun than a nosey kid sister, and minus the headaches. He often mused that money had been his most long-standing, dependable companion.

When his young dreams had been crushed along with his father's good mind, he'd leeched onto that friend with the fervor of a party boy on Bourbon Street. He'd taken any amount of his family's fortune his heart desired and purchased whatever his broken heart wanted, only to realize at the tender age of fifteen a lesson most adults never learn – that no amount of money or worldly indulgences could replace what he needed most: a father.

The lesson never left him, and he'd been diligent in his care of the family fortune ever after.

He'd come to thrive on seeking opportunities where he could lend a hand.

Rebekah's needs played in the back of his mind, as light and ethereal as her sweet nonsensical mutterings. He drove straight home, the exigency familiar and strong to lend a helping hand.

Nothing pleased him more than being able to ease another's burdens, a fact he knew those in his past – people like Lauren – were unaware of. He preferred it that way. He didn't need to feel the pat on his back from those whose lives he could assist. There was far greater satisfaction in knowing they would wonder, and never know.

Lauren's security system had been a given. This next

deed would never be tied to him and it brought a grim smile to his face. Grim only because he wished Rebekah was free of the disability of autism and didn't need special schooling to begin with.

He pulled in the circular drive of the spacious all-brick one-story home he had built after he'd returned from Princeton. The house was quiet when he entered, but in his mind he could still hear Rebekah's soft murmurings. He could see Lauren's image, the loving way she patiently cared for the little girl. It kept a smile on his lips.

He pushed up his sleeves and filed through the stack of mail his housekeeper, Mrs. Fuentes, always left on the granite counter top in the kitchen.

Alex took the mail to his office, a spacious room with dark wood trim in diamond-patterned beams across the ceiling. His love of books had prevented any wall space from being left in anything but floor-to-ceiling shelves, and those were stuffed to overflowing.

He'd gone through stages of interest in his life, and most of them were evident now in the shelves of this room. Some stages, like his intense interest in the brain, after what had happened to his father, garnered larger sections of shelving than passing fancies, such as Italian cooking. After he'd fumbled four attempts at Eggplant Parmesan, he'd chalked the rubbery stuff up to experience and moved on to other studies.

Dialing the black, high-tech speakerphone sitting on his desk, he lowered himself into the fat, tufted leather chair.

"Hello?"

"Driscol, it's Alex. I hope I'm not calling at a bad time." Though Alex was sure his lawyer would drop just about anything to talk to him, he would never presume.

"No, just finishing up some paper work. What can I do for you? Everything all right? Your mother, she's okay?"

"She's doing very well, thank you. I want you to look into Giant Steps. It's a private school for children with autism here in the area."

"I've a niece whose daughter attends there."

Alex was reminded of the shocking statistic Lauren had shared with him earlier that evening. "Really?"

"She's been going there for three years. Why?"

"I want to know what they need in the way of supplies and donations that would open up a spot for a friend of mine."

"Yes, but I know they have a full waiting list."

"She can't wait. Time is crucial. And she's young. She needs to get in there when it can really benefit her."

"You're right. The earlier they start intervention, the better. I can find out for you. How soon do you need to know?"

"As soon as possible. In fact, if you can get us an opening, let's take it. See what they're after, make them an offer and see if they'll take it. Use what you have to. I don't care what it is – new computers, a deluxe playground, specialty equipment – whatever. I want that place decked out like Disneyland."

"Will do. Mighty generous of you, Alex." The slip of emotion in Driscol's voice caused a band to tighten around Alex's chest. He'd known the man for twenty years and had no idea he had a relative with autism. "I know my niece would be thrilled at a windfall like this."

"Let's hope the powers that be at Giant Steps see it that same way."

After he'd hung up the phone, Alex felt the rush of his

nerves begin to settle. It was always a physical reaction like this, once he'd gotten a ball rolling. As if a great tide had finally broken, and was at last to free to flow.

Reclining back in the chair, he pressed his fingertips to his lips and felt the soft heat of her taste from that kiss earlier melt through his senses.

She'd be dancing now. He glanced at his watch, saw that only ten minutes remained of her rehearsal with Chad and Reuben. He closed his eyes, easily conjuring her in beaded sapphire from creamy shoulders to tantalizing calves, the way he longed to see her in performance or competition.

That was a laugh and he knew it. He really didn't care what she wore. Sure she had been gifted with an incredible body that had haunted his thoughts since high school, but there was so much more to her.

The portfolio of costumes sat on his desk and he sat forward, opening it. Their first competition would be in March, at Nationals. The costumes would be showstoppers. The pleasant hum he felt in his blood coiled into his stomach. He couldn't wait to see her, to cheer for her and watch her and Chad shock the judges and the audience.

He could think of her now and not feel envy at her dazzling capabilities. Part of him owned part of her, and that unity made their purpose one.

He sat back again, a smile on his lips. One in purpose – it had always been his father's philosophy for marriage, family and work. Only part of him was still empty. Half of him needed the completion he was searching for in companionship. Pulling inside now was the desire for children, a friend and lover – a wife with whom he could share this quiet house. If he had his way, this sponsorship would only be the beginning. He meant to have Lauren in every way a man could have a woman, and the thought spun the hum in his blood into a whirl he knew wouldn't slow.

With a laugh, he took himself to his bedroom and stripped for an icy shower.

twenty

It was a dream come true, the phone call from Giant Steps. Lauren wondered why suddenly it seemed things were going her way. She didn't consider herself a pessimist though lately she found herself fighting the dark gravitational pull. She fought back with the tooth and nail of drive and will.

But she'd never expected a respite from that fight so soon.

Now, she and Rebekah were on their way for Rebekah's first day at the special school. Lauren was sure this step would open doors in her little girl's brain. Since God seemed to be blessing her, Lauren would wish and hope and pray that this was just the beginning.

The old brick building looked as if it wept for its innocent occupants, gray mortar seeping down the red masonry. The spacious grounds were vacant of children; only ancient oaks towered protectively, like wrinkled grandparents hovering.

Programs like this were rarely housed in brand new, state of the art buildings, rather swept into corroded corners. At the risk of sounding ungrateful, Lauren told herself not to think like that. She was lucky to be there, moldy building and all.

At least it's clean inside, she thought. It wasn't freshly painted, but the walls and ceilings were white and spotless but for the dark wood work. She guessed it had been built around nineteen hundred. The official brass plaque of the Utah Historical Society hung on the outside of the double glass doors.

The distant mewling cries from the children greeted them. Lauren's shoes echoed in the empty hall as she led Rebekah to the office. The door was open. Sun poured from the only window, filling the room. Tiffany, the school coordinator, was on the phone. Her dark auburn hair pulled back, a pair of black glasses propped on the tip of her nose. She smiled and waved them in.

New places were always a challenge for Rebekah. She had to explore every inch before she would stop for a breath. She began climbing on one of the two chairs Tiffany had facing her desk.

"Time to sit, angel." Lauren plucked Rebekah from the chairs and sat then, wrapping Rebekah in a snug hold on her lap. In protest, Rebekah squirmed and grunted.

"Yes," Tiffany said into the phone. "I'll start putting a list together this morning. Yes. That's very generous. Thank you so much, I really can't thank you enough. Yes, they are great children, and these improvements will mean a lot for them. Thank you. Bye."

Tiffany's green eyes glittered. She hung up the phone. "You made it."

"Here we are." Lauren adjusted Rebekah's weight on her lap. "You sound like you've had a stroke of good luck as well."

"It seems to be in the air," Tiffany said. "I'm so glad Rebekah can join us." She stood and came around the desk, looking right at Rebekah. "Hello, Rebekah. I'm Tiffany. Do you remember me?"

For a scant moment Rebekah's blue eyes stayed with Tiffany's, but there was no sign of recognition. She squirmed to free herself. "I've looked over the paperwork you filled out, and I called the district and requested their reports. I know she's had some one-on-one work, but at Giant Steps we start all of our students in attending. They work up, passing off each needed skill before going on to the next."

"She can always use the reinforcement," Lauren said. "But once she passes off, she won't be held back just because she hasn't been here very long, will she?"

"If she passes off attending skills at ninety percent, ninety percent of the time, she'll move up. Every skill is documented and tracked. The data is what we go by, not time or parent's wishes."

"I understand." If wishes were all it took, Lauren knew for a fact, none of these kids would be here. "We all want the same thing."

"I know you've been told over and over to be realistic. We can't promise anything. Too many times I've seen kids that I thought wouldn't do anything come out like a racehorse, while others that looked like they were making progress stalled."

Please don't let that be Rebekah, Lauren pleaded in her heart. But she had so little control over it. She knew what she could do, provide as many opportunities as she was able, then let Rebekah – and fate – do the rest.

"Why don't we take Rebekah into Room One? That's where our teachers work on attending." Tiffany led them out into the hall. "From there the children move onto Room Two, where beginning academics takes place. Room Three is for the advanced learning skills. We also have a wonderful speech therapist and, with any luck, we'll have our own OT therapist soon."

It was loud in Room One. Adult voices sprung through the air like sharp arrows. Eight children sat in chairs with teachers facing them. Each teacher held a small plastic cup with bite-size treats for reinforcement. No one noticed that they entered, the teachers engrossed in holding the children's attention. The children watched as the instructor animatedly carried out the commands of attending, urging the children to look them in the eye and sit with their feet and hands down.

"Since you're familiar with the attending protocol, I won't explain the procedures. Kristin will be working with Rebekah. She's been working with children with autism for three years, and she's really good."

Tall, bouncy, dark-freckled from head to toe, Kristin swung up from working with a dark-haired little boy and shook Lauren's hand, then dipped to her knees to look Rebekah in the eye.

"Hello, Rebekah." Not expecting a response, Kristin clapped loudly, instantly bringing the child's eyes to hers. "Good looking at me when I talk to you. Good job, Rebekah. My name is Kristin." She stood then, still studying the little girl while she spoke to Lauren. "She's such a cutie. Has she had any attending?"

"Some."

"Good. Well, if she's ready, she can start."

Lauren felt a lump in her throat, and the familiar fluttering of fear she experienced when she left Rebekah somewhere new, trusting her baby to the care of others. "She's ready."

Kristin swooped down and picked her up. "Hey, she'll let me hold her, that's great. So many of the kids hate being touched. Come on then, Bekah. Is it okay if I call her Bekah?"

The term of endearment softened the sharp edges of apprehension gouging Lauren's heart. "Sure." She quickly kissed her daughter's soft cheek before Kristin had her in a seat right next to the dark-haired little boy who had been sitting, flapping his arms.

"She'll be fine." Tiffany laid a calming hand on Lauren's tense arm.

"Separation anxiety." Lauren patted her breastbone with a mother's sigh. "You'd think I'd be anxious to have some time to myself and that will be nice. But – it's never easy leaving her somewhere."

Tiffany gently guided her from the room. "Just because your child has a handicap doesn't mean you aren't entitled to some enjoyment of your own."

"Somehow the handicap makes it harder." Lauren heard the door close behind her. She and Tiffany walked down the empty hall and she wondered if Rebekah noticed or even cared that she had gone.

It never got easier not feeling the love she craved reciprocated from her own flesh and blood, living with the walls that kept Rebekah's heart and soul sheathed from the rest of the world. Times like this were pointed reminders of Lauren's relationship being more a stewardship than motherhood.

"About the monthly tuition," Lauren began as they returned to the office. "I know when I signed the waiting list I checked that I couldn't pay for it but that's changed."

"Yes, it has," Tiffany smiled.

"It has?"

"We just received a very generous donation and some of it will be offered in the way of scholarships. I took the liberty of signing you up for one, if you'd like. It would be a full-ride."

Lauren's eyes widened. "That would be wonderful."

"I thought that might help."

"But maybe there's someone else who needs it more. I can pay now, if there is."

Tiffany shook her head. "We'll take care of them as well."

The day couldn't get any better, Lauren thought. If she were dreaming, she would roll over and pull her pillow over her head and never move.

"If you'll just sign a few more pesky papers for me, I can let you get back to your day."

Lauren drove home and the quiet emptiness of the car urged tears to her eyes. The engine hum was a poor substitute for Rebekah's light mutterings. She couldn't look over her shoulder and see her little girl's smile, even if that smile was not for her. Not easily brought to tears, Lauren almost reached for the radio but thought better of it. She knew too well that indulging in the endowment of a silent moment could open her mind and heart unlike anything else.

Had she done the right thing, enrolling Rebekah at Giant Steps? Why she was questioning, she couldn't fathom. It had been what she'd wanted ever since she'd discovered the facility a few months ago. Perhaps it was all of the good fortune she was having after such a dry spell replete with hopeless cracks and deep lonely caverns that caused her puzzlement.

She had the day to herself now, not something she was used to and for a moment, she wasn't sure what to do. She'd made no plans, as if in her heart she'd not really believed her good fortune.

Her classes didn't start until four. She'd already arranged

for Aubrey to pick Rebekah up at Giant Steps because she would be in the middle of teaching. Then she had another rehearsal at eight with Reuben and Chad.

She wondered if Alex would be there. It had been days since she'd seen him, since that night he'd kissed her. It had been two years and six months since she'd been kissed – not that counting shamed her. She missed it.

Sparkling fire shot through her body remembering how Alex had taken charge of the moment they'd shared on the couch. She'd never been so thoroughly kissed, and with such expertise she wondered just how many other women Alex had possessed. Even if she wouldn't allow herself to have a relationship with Alex, that didn't mean she liked that he'd been around. What she liked was the idea of his sexuality being such a force that he couldn't contain it.

Her heart started fluttering, her body filled with need to touch him again. "Listen to you," she told herself as she pulled into her driveway. "You sound like a love-starved blank head." If she didn't do something, she'd be frustrated and ready to pop.

She could clean, though cleaning was something she only did because she had to. She could spend time in the yard, weeding. Having concocted a plan to derail the desire building for Alex, she enjoyed a moment of relief.

"Thinking like this about Alex Saunders," she muttered, taking the front walk to her door. "Are you out of your mind?"

Unlocking her door, she waited to hear the dinging sound of the chime. When it didn't signal, she opened the control panel with a frown. "Already it's not working?"

She really had no idea what could be wrong with it, but she pressed the button marked chime and the trouble light lit.

Expelling a sigh, she let her purse slip from her arm to the floor and grabbed her phone.

Damian's card was still on the kitchen counter and she dialed him.

"Hello?" His voice had a tuneful, expectant tone to it. Lauren stood in front of the panel perturbed. "Damian, it's Lauren Peay."

"Well, hello there."

"Yeah, hi. Um, something's wrong with my chime."

He let out a soft, low snicker. "There's nothing's wrong with any part of you, Lauren. Take my word for it."

"I'm talking about the alarm."

"Mmm, yeah."

She didn't appreciate the innuendo. "When I walked in just now, it didn't chime."

"You know, you're in luck. I'm in the neighborhood. Why don't I just come on by and take a look at it."

Though her stomach crimped with warning, she agreed, telling herself not to be paranoid. "That would be great."

"Be there in a minute," he said.

She hung up the phone unable to dislodge the wariness she felt. "This is silly," she checked out the front window for his truck. "He's an old acquaintance. There's no reason to get uptight."

Because Rebekah had dropped a few toys and clothes about, she picked up, the act serving to settle her nerves with the habit. It took her mind to her child, to what she would be doing in that new place, to whether or not Rebekah was afraid being somewhere unfamiliar, with strangers.

One of the conundrums Lauren disliked most about autism was that the children often didn't show preference for anything. There was little difference between stranger and friend.

Lauren set the toys and clothes in Rebekah's room just as she heard Damian's knock on the door.

"Hey," she greeted him as if he was Mr. Rogers, the safest guy in the neighborhood.

"Lauren." He dipped his head with a serpent smile that, in spite of her Mr. Rogers efforts, slithered straight to her gut.

The scent of strong cologne filled her nose when he entered. He must have it in his truck, she mused, knowing most scents died after a few hours' wear. He glanced around the room casually and she wondered why. He knew very well where the control panel was.

"The trouble light went on suddenly." She tapped on the panel to get his attention.

"Let's see here." Setting down his case, he whipped out a tiny screwdriver and removed the face of the panel revealing an orderly set of multi-colored wires and other electronic pieces. "Hmm."

She kept her eyes on what he was doing over his shoulder while he fiddled with the wires. Someone she had dated once had worn the strong scent, and she hadn't liked the guy. But how shallow are you to judge someone because of his taste in cologne or perfume? When Damian turned his head and smiled at her, she made the extra effort and smiled back.

"Faulty wire." He tugged out a tiny red wire with what looked like large tweezers. "I'll replace it and it will be as good as new."

She laughed. "It is new."

His laugh joined hers. "Sorry about that. These panels are pre-made. Never can tell what the Chinese were doing when they put them all together. Probably high…or drunk."

Lauren refrained from making a comment. He squatted down, rummaged through his box and brought out a tiny plastic bag of red wires wrapped like half a pretzel.

His hair was golden brown and spiked into place with a good deal of mousse. Damian was a man who cared about how he looked when he walked out the front door, she could tell. His gray uniform was perfectly ironed and clean. Only the faint odor of stale cigarette gave away a nasty habit.

"When did you take up smoking?" she asked.

He looked up, taken aback and a little embarrassed. "Guess my cologne's not working." Then he stood, looking down into her eyes with a playful grin. "Turn you off?"

She shrugged, and crossed her arms over her chest. He wasn't unattractive by any shot, but not her type. Something about him put her off, though she repeatedly told herself her fear wasn't based on anything substantial. She could hardly blame an old high school prank for her misgivings. That was juvenile. Just as she had put aside her negative feelings for Alex, she should do the same for Damian.

"You dating anybody right now?" he asked before he moved back to the panel.

"That was random." She didn't want to sound available, and figured a lie was acceptable in this case. "I see someone off and on." It was perfectly fine to say, in light of the fact that Lauren was using her partnership with Chad at the moment.

"Seriously?" He kept his dark eyes on her as he worked.

"Not seriously." Lauren shifted.

"How long has Saunders been sniffing around? Not that I blame him." He moved closer to her. "I wouldn't mind giving it a try. A drink? Maybe dinner?"

"You said you gave up drinking."

"Yeah, but I'd be the last person to deny anybody else the sultry pleasure."

"Uh." Flashes of that night in the parking lot raided Lauren's mind. Of boys' laughter, and breath that reeked of stale beer. She hoped she hadn't paled. "I'm pretty busy, but thanks for the offer."

He got back to the panel, seemingly unaffected by the rejection. "I'd be disappointed if you were still afraid of me, Lauren."

She lifted her chin as a shudder overtook her. "Of course I'm not afraid of you."

"Good." He eyed her. "Because I want to do more than replace your faulty wires." He closed the panel, wiped his hands and faced her. "What's it going to take?"

"I – I just told you that I'm busy."

He let out a laugh. "Come on, you eat don't you? I saw you eat with Saunders. And I can promise a hell of a lot nicer place than McDonalds. Let me take you out."

She had serious doubts that she could keep any food down sitting across the table from him during a meal. She would be too nervous. "I'm rehearsing every free minute I have, Damian."

"I'd like to see you dance again." His voice lowered a pitch. "Like to see how perfection improves itself."

"I'm far from the perfect dancer." Lauren felt a snow job coming. "Done?" She purposefully nodded at the panel behind him.

"Oh." He let out a laugh. "Yeah…with the panel." Slowly he moved toward her, his eyes lively. "I'm serious about taking you out, Lauren."

"I can see that. But I can't do dinner or lunch or breakfast for that matter. When I'm not teaching, I'm rehearsing or competing. And like you, I have a child. Only, unlike you, she lives with me. And she has autism."

A flash of soberness daunted his eyes then. "I'd heard that, yeah. How is she doing?"

Because she saw real concern on his face, she forgot his pursuance and opened her heart. "Pretty well. But that's why I had the alarm installed. A few weeks ago she opened her bedroom window and ran."

"Just took off? Out of the blue?"

"A lot of kids with autism run. Nobody really knows why, except that it's some kind of stim for them."

"Stim?"

Lauren never tired of explaining autism. She figured the more people she could help educate, the more accepting the world would be of her daughter and children like her. "Self-stimulating. You've probably seen or heard of children with autism flapping? That's one way of stimming. They're very controlled by their appetite to stimulate themselves." She knew how it sounded, and half expected Damian to make some tasteless sexual joke. She was impressed when he didn't.

"Wild," he said. "I don't know anything about it. So I guess the alarm will help buy you some peace of mind then."

"That's why Alex had it installed for me."

A mix of suspicion and curiosity was on his face. "And you want me to believe you're not seeing him?"

"Not dating him, Damian. I see him."

"Boy," he laughed. "That must be driving him crazy."

"Why? We're just friends."

"Uh – yeah. That's lucky for me then. Listen, since you

won't let me take you out to eat any meal, how about you let me come watch you dance?"

Lauren would rather say goodbye – permanently. Some men were impossibly blind, unable to see rejection for what it was. For that reason, she figured a rehearsal would at least be harmless. "I rehearse every night at the studio from eight to ten."

Damian picked up his steel case and extended his hand to shake but when she slipped her hand in his, he deftly lifted it to his lips and placed a slow, hot kiss on her knuckles.

The kiss flew through her with a turbulent mix of fear that stunned. "Until then."

She watched him stride to his truck, one hand confidently in his front pocket, the other clutching the metal case before she shut the door, pressing her forehead against it. She slowed her panicked breath.

She turned, her back against the door, and let out a groan.

Testing the door for the chime, she looked out where his truck was just pulling away. She was making far too much of this. She'd firmly told him she was not interested in anything and he'd accepted graciously. Her invitation was nothing, really, an acquaintance extending herself to another acquaintance. Not even that.

"It's just a rehearsal." She went back to picking up.

twenty-one

Rehearsal had gone without a hitch. Lauren caught herself staring at her and Chad's reflection in the wall of mirrors as they danced. Reuben's careful watch for details had really paid off. He chatted during their ten-minute break with Alex. The two men sat with their heads tight, laughing occasionally. Lauren was curious what they could be talking about, but her professionalism wouldn't give Alex even a hint that she cared personally.

"We're hot." Chad took a sip from his water bottle, his eyes gleaming with youthful exuberance. "We're looking so freaking good, I can't believe it."

She smiled. "Things have improved, yes. Don't get too cocky, it's bad luck."

"I have every right to be cocky." He wiped his brow with his forearm. "I'm dancing with Lauren Peay, ranked twenty-fifth in the world."

"Very flattering, but we're basically starting over, you know that. We still have to establish our own name and rank."

He lifted a shoulder. "Easy."

Most dancers were confident, and if they weren't, they never let it show. It was all part of sportsmanship. In her life as a competitor, Lauren had felt that smooth joy of perfection once before, when she and Peter had danced, and won.

While she admired Chad's thick-with-pride blinders, she hoped he kept at least a glance of realism somewhere. They'd been to one competition and placed, but Nationals would be their first introduction as a new partnership into the

Dancing With His Heart - Katherine Warwick

international ballroom world. They would need to be beyond perfect to compete with the other couples she knew would provide them with hefty opposition.

Their costumes would be unbeatable. She stole a glance at Alex through the mirror.

His eyes met hers and she quickly looked away, shrugging out the tension just looking at him rammed through her body. She'd gotten over the initial disconcertion of having him watch. After that kiss, she found herself anxious to see if he would be at every rehearsal, sitting on the sidelines in one of his expensive designer outfits. He always was.

He never took his eyes from her, and that added an extra punch to her performance, knowing he wanted her. Why else would he be there? That kiss had been hungry, a starved lion finally free of its cage. Remembering shot a sweet shudder through her middle and she looked at him again, and found his predatory gaze still following her.

She tilted her head at him.

Why was it so satisfying to tease and tempt him? she wondered, now walking back and forth in front of the mirror as she cooled down. There was power in it, and power was something they both fought hard for. Fighting each other for it was hot, sexy and irresistible. Lauren added the tiniest sway to her hips as she walked, heating inside because Alex shifted in his chair.

The door to the studio swung open and Damian sauntered in. Lauren stopped in her tracks, her bottom lip drawn taut between her teeth. The conversation between Reuben and Alex ceased, throwing a thick blanket of silence across the room.

Damian wore khaki slacks and a snug, long-sleeved navy

188

tee shirt showcasing his well-muscled chest and arms.

"Damian." She'd hoped just the invitation to observe the rehearsal would have appeased him. To see him there surprised her. Forcing herself to cordiality, she lifted her chin with a performer's smile. Out the corner of her eye Alex snapped to attention, his angry energy electrifying the room. "You decided to join us."

"Couldn't pass up the invitation." Damian sauntered over and covered her hand with his, holding it just long enough that it brought Alex over.

"Damian." Alex didn't even reach out to shake his hand. "What are you doing here?"

Allowing his appreciative smile to linger on Lauren, Damian kept her hand captured. "Lauren invited me." Then he gently kissed her knuckles.

"Yes." She tugged her hand free before turning briefly to Alex. "He wanted to watch."

Alex sneered, "I'll bet he did."

"Good to see you too, old buddy." Damian patted Alex's shoulder quickly then strolled over to Reuben and Chad with his hand out. "Damian. I'm an old friend of Lauren's. And Alex's."

"Cool." Chad shook his hand enthusiastically.

"Reuben." After shaking Damian's hand, Reuben gestured to the seats. "If you came to watch, you're just in time. We're getting back to work, aren't we kids?" Reuben clapped his hands, his standard signal that it was time to get down to business.

Damian made himself comfortable on one of the chairs, sending a wide grin to Alex.

"You invited him?" Alex whispered to her.

"We'll talk about this later."

"When? When did you invite him?"

"The other day."

Alex's jaw hardened. "What, did he call you?"

"I said we'll talk about this later." She turned to join Chad, but he had her by the elbow.

He waited until her glare met his before releasing her. It was all Alex could do not to implode. Astounded that Lauren had invited Damian, but worse, shocked that the two of them had had contact without his knowledge.

Alex tore his stare away from Lauren just long enough to glare at Damian as he took the seat next to him. The ravenous look in Damian's eyes set every muscle in his body on edge.

"I don't know what you think you're doing, but I'll warn you again," Alex's voice sliced like a blade of steel. "Stay away from her."

Damian sat back and stretched out his arms along the chairs with a confident grin. "You don't own her, Saunders."

Reuben put on the music, a fast-tempo of cymbals and guitars, of sensual drums and tart violins. As soon as Lauren started to move, Alex's throat went dry. With Damian watching, his feelings of possession ruptured. He had to keep himself from lunging across the floor and wrapping around Lauren's lithe body so that Damian wouldn't have the satisfaction of seeing her.

Pinned to the chair, unable to stop her hips from churning, her arms from beckoning, Alex began to sweat. Next to him, Damian enjoyed the performance as if the two of them were sitting stage-side at a nightclub show. More than anything, Alex wanted to wrap his fists around Damian's shirt and throw the letch out.

But Lauren had invited him; and he wanted to know why. Was she attracted to the man? It seemed so illogical; Alex would have laughed if rage hadn't choked on disappointment in his throat.

Whatever game Lauren was playing with Damian, he felt sure she had no idea how dangerous it was. That she liked danger hadn't bothered him – until now. She was dancing too close to the altar for his liking. No way was he going see her sacrificed at the hands of a loose wire like Damian.

"She's fabulous." Damian leaned over to Alex.

The compliment scratched at Alex's exposed ego. "Yes, she is."

"Hot. Very hot," Damian murmured, then slid Alex an amused grin. "You must have it bad to be panting at her heels like you are. Pretty hard to take 'no', isn't it, old buddy?"

"She hasn't had to say no to me," Alex began tightly. "We have a business arrangement."

That seemed to amuse Damian even more. "And you're settling for that? Times must be hard. I remember a day when you could have any woman you wanted, whenever you wanted. I guess that just proves that even rich guys can't have it all."

Alex's jaw began to ache. If he opened it, said one more word to Damian, he'd pop the lid off something that could very well turn nasty for them both. If they'd been alone he would have ripped Damian's smug smile from his face. But they were observing a rehearsal of his star couple, and nothing would offend Lauren more than to see him lose control and get into a juvenile fight.

"You make one move her direction and I'll be there to stop you."

"My, oh, my." Damian let out a laugh that filled the

room, even over the raucous Latin music. It brought all eyes to him. "Does she know that you're in love with her?"

Alex's face heated. He glanced at Lauren who hadn't heard Damian's comment over the music. She continued dancing with Chad.

"You're in love with her, aren't you? Or do you just want to—"

Alex snagged Damian's shirtfront then, and dragged his face to his. "You let that weasel brain of yours even think of her that way and I'll throw you out of here."

Damian's dark eyes flared with challenge. He set his fingers over Alex's to unwrap the grip. "Too late, I've thought about it."

Alex shot up, every fiber taut with adrenalin. He jerked his head toward the door. "Outside. Now."

Damian didn't make a move, rather stretched out again, setting his gaze back on Lauren who had been distracted enough by their raised voices that she stopped and stood watching.

When his star pupils stopped dancing, Reuben turned the music down, aware of something turbulent happening between Alex and Damian.

"Everything cool?" he asked.

Damian nodded, his white teeth gleaming. "Everything's just fine. Don't stop on our account. Baby, you are absolutely incredible."

Lauren's face showed her confusion. "Thank you."

"You okay, bro?" Reuben looked at Alex standing threateningly over Damian.

It took a minute for Alex to accept that Damian had won this round with control. More control than he had, and he sat back down rigidly, hiding defeat.

Alex knew one thing for certain; he had to convince Lauren that whatever she was doing with Damian had to stop. Why she didn't take his word for it dispirited him, made him realize he stood absolutely nowhere when it came to importance in Lauren's life, or she would listen to him.

He'd have rather been hung on a rack and eaten alive. The torture of watching her dance was just as wretched. Alex wondered how he would ever make it through countless competitions without wanting to rip into every judge that didn't give her high scores. Pull the lustful eyes out of every man in the audience. Only one thing would settle this roving, untamed need to possess her – he had to have her.

The two-hour rehearsal wound him into an unbreakable coil. He watched that shapely, tight body of hers, covered only in a thin veil of black, bend, dip, twist and writhe to the thudding music until it nearly broke him.

When Reuben at last turned off the music, Alex's whole being sighed. Forcing himself to cool off, he thought about how he would proceed. Coming on like a bulldozer without breaks was not going to appeal to Lauren. That he could bet on. There was no way he was going to sit back and take it while she pranced around with Damian. Her silly rule about not mixing business with pleasure would have to change.

And then there was Damian's allegation. "*Does she know that you're in love with her?*" The thought wouldn't leave him, and he knew why – because it was the truth. It had taken the perception of an old friend for him to see it, to admit it to himself. Alex wondered if it was that obvious. Had Lauren any idea?

He hung back, allowing Reuben the time to confer with

his dancers before officially ending rehearsal. Damian kept his distance as well, a smart move for both of them, Alex decided, even though he kept a watchful eye on the man. It seemed to Alex that Damian was ready to pounce from the sidelines like a hyena.

Even more difficult than watching Lauren dance was holding back when Reuben and Chad left, and watching Damian saunter over to her.

"You were awesome." Damian was all smiles as he approached.

Lauren had yet to stop sweating, and where it never bothered her, she didn't care for Damian's eyes traveling thirstily over her bare, wet skin. "Thank you."

"Seriously, I'm floored. You two sizzle."

Why Alex stood back quietly made her wonder. Grabbing a towel out of her duffle, she started dabbing at herself.

"Let me take you out for something to eat. Or drink. From the looks of you, I'll bet you're parched."

"Uh, thank you, but I already have plans." She had hoped that whatever fantasy he had of the two of them would be appeased after the dance.

"Too bad." Damian reached out and lifted a strand of fallen hair from her face. The gesture caused her eyes to widen. Quickly, she smiled and made a casual cross to the music. She put on something downbeat, something she felt sure Damian would not like. Johnny Mathis.

He didn't have a reaction one way or another to the music, and joined her. "How about you to teach me how to dance?"

"I don't teach adults." It wasn't the truth, of course.

Lauren had taught countless private lessons to people of every age. Over his shoulder, Lauren could see Alex slowly heading their direction.

"Not even old friends?"

She tilted her head at him. "Let's not stretch the truth, Damian. You're more than welcome to talk to Stephanie or Jill. They teach the adult standard and Latin ballroom classes."

He shook his head, closing the space between them. "I want to take from the best."

"They're both excellent teachers."

"But they're not you."

Lauren glanced at Alex, drawing closer now, and couldn't help that she felt relief.

He stopped just behind Damian. "Well, it looks like you two need some privacy," Alex's smile was oddly artificial. "Lauren, great work tonight." Then he started toward the door. "I'll call you over the next few days."

Panic shot through her. He was leaving? She would be alone with Damian. "Uh, Alex, don't leave just yet."

He stopped and turned, casually jangling his keys.

"He was just on his way out," Damian's tone was lined with annoyance. "I can help you lock up."

"It's not that." Lauren started toward Alex. "We have some business that can't wait."

Alex angled his head at her as she approached. A faint smile played on his lips. "Do we?"

She nodded, reached out and took his hand. "Important business."

Damian shoved his hands in his front pockets and rocked back on his heels, tongue in his cheek. "I see. Well, guess that's my cue." Even though Lauren still held onto Alex's hand like a life preserver, he stole her free hand and kissed it. "Thank you for allowing me to watch you dance. A pleasure."

As soon as her hand was free, she said, "You're welcome."

"Sure you won't change your mind and teach me some moves?"

"I'm afraid I haven't the time."

He nodded cordially at Alex. "Alex. I'm sure we'll be seeing each other."

"Don't count on it." Instinctively, Alex tugged Lauren close. Damian cocked a brow at the move, then crossed the floor, his shoes echoing. The heavy metal door slammed behind him.

twenty-two

Lauren let out a relieved sigh and closed her eyes. Thankfully, that was over. When her eyes opened, she found herself staring at Alex. His posture was rigid, the planes and angles of his face drawn taut with something she wasn't sure she could read. But he didn't look happy.

Her hand still held his and she looked at it – at them – joined. She tried to swallow the knot in her throat, but it wouldn't go down.

Johnny Mathis was singing about the Twelfth of Never, and everything around them warmed to the mellow, sweet melody.

She wanted to thank him for staying and saving her from what would have been an embarrassing exercise in rejection. But something furious flashed in his eyes, and before she knew it, she was against him, his arm around her waist in a grip that nearly stole her breath.

"What was that all about?" he demanded.

"What?"

"Maybe you didn't hear me when I told you to stay away from Damian. He's poison. Or do you like sticking your neck out? You want to get bitten, Lauren? Is that it?"

Infuriated, she wriggled to free herself, but he held her pinned. When she reached up to push at him, he caught her swing with his other hand. "Let me go." Heat reddened her cheeks as she struggled against him.

"Not until you tell me what's going on."

His arms were the branches of an oak, wrapped around

her waist without mercy. Sparks lit inside of her and her knees weakened. Part of her wanted this, to be dominated and controlled. To fight, yes, but then to savor the sweetness of surrender.

Her breath came in fast, and he stole a glance at the way her breasts heaved against his chest. She felt the slightest give in his grip – a weakening she meant to take advantage of, and pushed free. She was surprised when he released her.

They faced each other in swirling silent heat.

"Nothing's going on with Damian," she started, her voice low and husky. His eyes flickered at the sound of it. "My alarm wasn't working. He came over to fix it and wanted to take me out. I didn't want that. So I invited him to rehearsal hoping to get him off my back. Satisfied?"

"You let him touch you. He kissed your hand."

"What was I supposed to do? Slap him?"

He jerked out a nod. "Or slug him. Either would have worked."

"He was—"

"Coming onto you, and I don't like it." He was flush against her again, his eyes spearing into hers. "I don't want him near you."

Alarm chased the anger out of her heart. He was completely serious. She could no more deny the pleasure that gave her, than refute her growing feelings for him. They were interminably entwined. Drawing her lower lip between her teeth, she remained silent, unsure of what to say, of what his command really meant. Ambiguous as his statement was, stirring inside of her was the need to press for complete understanding. Her gaze remained locked with his.

"Why don't you want him near me?"

He seemed caught up in the nearness of her and she reveled in that, enjoying his struggle to contain feelings dancing too close to the surface.

"I don't want—" he couldn't finish, and his vulnerability touched her.

"What?" she asked softly. "I thought this was about what you wanted, Alex."

"It is." He swallowed thickly, and stepped back, releasing her. He eyed her guardedly. "What about your plans?"

"Plans?"

"You told Damian you had plans."

"That was a detour meant to save him from an evening of embarrassment. Thank you, by the way, for stepping in."

"You're admitting that I helped you out of a tight spot?"

"I don't have a problem admitting that."

"What if I had left? You looked pretty sure of yourself."

"And I could have handled him."

Amused, he looked admiringly over her face, settling on her lips. "I bet you could have. It wasn't free. There's a price to pay."

She enjoyed a luscious shudder. "Forget it." And she turned; but he swung her around, and held her in dance position.

"Dance with me."

Feeling him next to her only served to remind her how perfectly they fit together. How wonderful it was to be held by someone other than a dance partner, to flirt with the possibilities of more than just dancing.

"I can't."

"I know you said you don't teach adults, but I'm telling you now to make an exception."

She cocked her head back. "Because you're the boss?" He smiled, nodded.

"There's no point in arguing, I suppose," she said, resigning herself to the fact that he had done her a favor and she could return in kind. "What dance do you want me to teach you?"

"Let's pick up where we left off."

"Tango then?" She eased away with a flirtatious swing in her step. "I'll have to change the music."

At last he was going to have her to himself. Alex's fingers dug anxiously into his hips as he stood waiting. She moved so fluidly, he was captivated. Liquid heat, both swift yet measured. Seductive. He couldn't wait to have his hands on her.

Something dark and exciting filled the air. Drums thudded quietly. Soon, a swoon of violins joined them. Cymbals, guitars. The strumming slowed, and Lauren came to him.

His heart flew wildly in his chest. She reached out, arms beckoning, and he thought if he could, he'd open up and let his heart free.

Her sweat-cooled flesh was under his hands. Flecks of gold lightened the dark emerald of her eyes. The scent of her filled his senses, clean and sweet.

"On my count." Her voice was a mystic lull, and he was helpless not to obey. "Slow, slow, quick, quick. Your thighs lock with mine, Alex, nice and tight." Her eyes teased, as if she knew how hard it was for him to hear her command his body to do things that would only entice him more.

Her pelvis fit his like two plates, stacked, and she pressed herself more closely to him. "Much better. Remember, in tango we're joined here." Her hand left his only for the moment it took to skim the hard contours of his lower abdomen. The light touch nearly burned him. "Easy, easy," she grinned. "You're too tight."

"Damn right," he almost growled. Confining his movement was too much to bear. He'd had enough of her body brushing his, of her waist twisting under his hands, her skin slipping and sliding, taunting fingers desperate to tear.

Yanking her against him, one arm held her captive while the other shoved ruthlessly into her hair. The shock on her face stirred his blood into a tremor that wracked his body, fast and hard. Her lips parted, moist, pink. Before she could utter a word, his hand fisted, pulling her head back, exposing her throat, a long pale path he was going to travel.

He could feel her heart racing against his and he licked his lips, anticipating the taste of her. Slowly, he lowered his mouth to skim the ivory silk that was the side of her neck. The instant his heat met hers, her body trembled, and he squeezed. He didn't want her to resist. She was his now, and he would do what he pleased.

Long, succulent kisses he laid along her throat, trailing her jaw, to her chin. He could see her eyes, wide, excited, anxious. They were sharing breath now, steaming gasps, in and out. Torment, that's what it was, her breath mingling with his, her lips brushing his tip to tip.

"Lauren." It was an urgent whisper. So much he wanted to say to her; so insignificant were his words. He cupped her cheeks, looking into her eyes. He'd never felt this way about a woman. No one had ever consumed him like this. No one could satisfy the fervent need he had for only her. He was willing to open his heart fully, to do something he had never done before and expose what was really inside of him to someone other than those close to him.

His cell phone buzzed in his pocket.

For a moment, he ignored it, enjoying the feel of her body, the shallowness of her breath. As his phone continued to squeal, the look in her eyes shifted from dreamy desire to alert concern.

"Your phone," she whispered. He watched her lips say it, then leaned, kissing them slow and deep again, pulling away leisurely enough that her mouth clung to his with wet heat.

One hand held the side of her face, the other reached into his front pocket, retrieving the phone. "This is Alex…"

Lauren kept her hand over his, finding his touch sweet and romantic. She would have easily pegged him a player, and maybe she was kidding herself. Perhaps those well-oiled moves weren't a result of what was inside as much as what he'd learned along the way.

Then she scolded her self for being so quick to judge. Hadn't she learned anything these past few weeks?

His face drew tight suddenly; the hand at her face fell to her shoulder. "I'll be right there. Yes. I'm just a few minutes away." He clicked off the phone.

When he didn't say a word, she knew something very serious had happened. His normally bronzed skin waxed pasty. She could feel his fingers digging into her shoulder.

"Alex, what?"

"I need to go." There was pleading in his voice, and it sluiced her heart. "Something's happened."

"What? Can you tell me?" She took his hand from her shoulder and held onto it. "Is there something I can do?"

He swallowed first, then took a hard breath. "Can you come with me? Do you have time? I know Rebekah-"

"Yes. Yes, I can come. I'll call Aubrey." She jogged over to her bag, dug into it as he headed toward the door.

He was quiet on the short drive. Lauren called Aubrey and arranged for her to stay until she got home. Alex maneuvered the car with the intensity of a racecar driver stuck in five o'clock traffic, one hand on the wheel, the other scraping the stubble of his jaw. Lauren wasn't sure what to say. Whatever had happened, she had a feeling it was bad.

After a while, he finally spoke, but he kept his eyes on the road. "My father." He said nothing more, but Lauren knew something was terribly wrong. When she and Alex were in school, she could only remember that something had happened to his father, but she couldn't remember what.

It had been years since she'd been to the Saunders estate, the last time being a joke between girlfriends when they had decided they would get back at him for all that he'd done to her and toilet paper the place. They'd taken one look at the sprawling grounds and decided not to take on the forest of trees and shrubs surrounding the massive brick colonial.

The circular drive took Alex's black BMW right to the double-wide front doors. Through a window over the front door Lauren saw an elegant chandelier with enough light to rival the sun.

Alex opened her door for her and kept his hand at her back as he rushed them through the front doors, past an elderly man who mumbled something Lauren couldn't understand, then up an elegant, winding stair.

The house was deathly silent. Lauren found herself on her tip toes, even on what felt like velvet carpet.

"This way," Alex whispered, his hand slipping from her back to her hand. His grip was tight and urgent, concern darkened his face. They walked down a long hall, lit only by lacy lights overhead.

The smell of hospital was Lauren's first clue. The room Alex led her into was dressed in brilliant floral wallpaper in deep jewel tones. Furnishings in rich mahogany and leather were scattered with utilitarian pieces from a hospital – an adjustable bed, a rolling table, and various machines.

Lauren's gaze settled immediately on the frail man lying propped in the bed, a single light glowing over his head. His mouth was open, not in need of breath but from the inability to keep it closed. A woman with black hair, pulled into a tight bun at the nape of her neck, sat on the bed with him, holding one of his hands.

Two men stood next to the bed. All of them turned when she and Alex entered. The woman with dark hair looked at her with dark eyes that mirrored Alex's. No expression changed her face, drawn tight with fear.

Alex at last let go of Lauren's hand and crossed to the bed, putting his arms around the woman. Her light sobs broke the quiet that hung in the air.

Lauren's heart banged against her ribs. She felt desperately out of place. For minutes that dragged across the fragile glass of hope and reality, life clung. She stood in the darkness of the room, taken by the uncertainty surrounding her.

Alex ran his hand comfortingly along his mother's head. "Let me kiss him," he told her. His mother clung to the fabric of his shirt. Finally, she eased back, and Alex cupped her face, wiping back her tears with his thumbs before he moved to his father.

Taking his father's frail hand, Alex held it as if it was a

broken bird. His head lowered to his chest only for a moment before lifting on a deep breath. Lauren wanted to slip out of the room, away from this very private moment, but he had asked her to come and she realized then that the request had had a purpose. He wanted her there.

He leaned slowly over, placing a soft kiss on his father's forehead. The gentle way he ran a hand along his father's fragile crown and cheek tore her heart. But when she saw his shoulders buckle, emotion stole up her throat and into her eyes. Her chest clutched and she had to fight tears spilling down her cheeks.

Alex murmured something in his father's ear and then turned, taking his mother against him again. For a long time they stood holding each other.

"Do you think he'll come back out of it?" his mother asked.

Alex nodded. "I'm sure of it." He cradled his mother against his chest, and his eyes met Lauren's. "It'll be all right."

twenty-four

Lauren waited in a large room filled with a collection of antiques and books. She imagined it was an office, a study, or maybe even a library with the extensive collection of books lining the walls.

After Alex had introduced her to his mother and the two male nurses who attended his father, she had offered to call a friend to come and get her, but Alex asked if she would please stay. So she had.

Having time to herself, she called Aubrey, made sure Rebekah was okay, then browsed the books she figured Alex had grown up with. Titles she had never heard of were mixed with classics, as well as modern fiction and non-fiction. The vast collection made her wonder which belonged to the man who now lay unable to enjoy them.

"They were my father's."

She turned and found Alex just in the door, a weary smile on his face. She had the sudden urge to comfort him. She took a step toward him when he approached. Her feelings for him were changing, and she had no control over the direction they were taking.

He let out a sigh as he neared, looking down into her eyes. "Thank you."

"I—" Inadequate words fluttered from her lips. "I haven't done anything."

"You were here, and I appreciate that."

"Is he all right?"

He nodded and took her hand. Warmth tingled where

his fingers held hers next to his heart. "What happened to him, Alex?"

"You didn't hear?"

She shook her head. He led her to a stuffed burgundy leather couch and after she sat, joined her. "When I was twelve, he was in a car accident. The way his head hit the steering wheel – the doctors said the odds were one in a million, but he lost everything."

"I'm so sorry."

"We've learned to live with it." He looked into her eyes. "As you well know, that journey can take a very long time."

It struck her then, he knew better than anyone that she understood what he meant. All this time she had thought he was like everybody else. The truth humbled her. "Why didn't you tell me?"

He lifted a shoulder. "It's not that I kept it from you, it never came up. We never talk about our families." He gave her hand a soft squeeze. "Except for Rebekah."

"You should have told me." She looked away a moment to hide frustration. She preferred it fair, and not knowing something vital made the field on which they were playing crooked.

With his finger, he turned her chin. "I didn't hold it back purposefully. It's not something I talk about with people that I don't trust implicitly."

The explanation stole her aggravation and replaced it with admiration and humility. That he would trust her enough to open his heart in that way surprised and pleased her, stealing any reply.

"That surprises you," he said, lips curving a little. "I can tell. Come on, Lauren. All this time, I thought I was being obvious."

"It was obvious that you wanted to control me, Alex, that's all I got."

He let out a laugh that eased the tension she'd seen on his face since they had arrived at the house. "That's all?" He inched closer. "You're still teasing, aren't you?" Cupping her face, her drew it close to his. The move shot sweet fluttering through her system. His eyes darkened. "You've always known how to get to me."

She started to quiver, wanting to feel his lips hot on hers again. The way his eyes devoured her made her willing to abandon herself to him right there, without question.

"There's more to all of this between you and me than that," he said. "I hope you can see that as well."

Fantasies flashed in her mind that she didn't dare dream could come true; caring, love, marriage. Home. Even if those pictures were only fabrications of her female delusional mind, she would savor them privately. In the meantime, here she was with this brilliant, romantic and complex man she was beginning to wonder if she would ever understand.

"You're the most intense man I've ever known," she murmured, lips inching toward his.

"You like that, don't you?" His breath fanned her mouth and she sucked it in, held it as her own and nodded. "You like a man that keeps you guessing. Makes you wonder. I've always known that about you."

"You have?"

It was his turn to nod. "Since that first time I saw you with those outrageous little bunny ear pony tails you used to do with your hair."

She smiled. "You mean the ones you tugged?"

"I couldn't help myself. I had to touch you." The look in his eye intensified. "I knew then that I wanted you."

The news shocked and stirred her. Even more than she wanted answers and truth, she couldn't wait to feel the pressure of him against her. "Kiss me," she whispered.

His lips curved as they came even closer.

She nearly melted. Her mouth anxiously sought his.

Though he could easily consume her right there on the couch, in the back of Alex's mind was the pressing issue of his father.

He enjoyed one last deep kiss before wrapping her in his arms, delighting that the kiss still shook her system, and he could feel it. He was glad beyond words she was there with him, wished even more she could stay.

"I need to get you back home," he whispered against her hair, then kissed her head.

"Is there anything I can do for you or your mother?"

He stood and drew her from the couch. "I can take care of her." Lifting her knuckles to his lips, he left a kiss on the back of her hand. "But there is one thing you can do for me."

She was afraid to ask; the look in his eyes sparkled with craving. Because she knew it would thrill her as much as it would excite him, she said, "Anything."

He shook his head, eyes smiling, scheming. "You can expect that request in the very near future, Lauren."

twenty-five

If she'd had dreams of him, Lauren couldn't remember, but the following day she woke with a smile on her face.

She floated through a wonderful morning and afternoon, and she supposed she could attribute her pleased mood to what was happening in her heart for Alex. Or that Tiffany had called and told her Rebekah was doing so well, they would be moving her to Room 2 within another week. She was getting along with the other students and though she had begun to imitate one of the louder children's screams, they had efficiently nipped that behavior in the bud. Nothing brightened Lauren's spirits like news of her child's progress.

Alex called and told her he would be bringing the gowns and Chad's costumes to rehearsal. She couldn't wait to see them.

It was nice having him call, even if it was for something necessary. Having a man to talk with after a long drought was like having a waterfall just at her fingertips. Hers was the decision to stand back or plunge in.

As she waited in the studio alone, she tamped powder on her chin and nose and touched up her lipstick. Looking into her own wide-eyed reflection, she hurriedly wiped off the light pink shell color in favor of leaving her lips bare for him.

What are you doing? She'd never been the kind to change for the whims of a man. Where Alex was concerned, she usually preferred creating obstacles.

When the door opened, her stomach lurched in anticipation. Only Chad and Reuben had walked in.

They started rehearsal immediately, going over every routine with a detailed precision. After going through all ten dances, Reuben's electrifying grin lit up the studio.

"You're ready, guys." He stood with them in the center of the room while they both caught their breaths. "It's hard to believe you've only been dancing together for a few months. Great work."

Lauren hadn't looked at the clock once, so immersed in rehearsing. But the hours had vanished, and she wondered where Alex was, surprised at the intensity of her curiosity.

With a family waiting for him at home, Reuben never stuck around after lessons, and tonight was no different. He kissed Lauren on the cheek, shook Chad's hand and admonished them to give it a rest for the night.

"I thought we were going to check out the costumes." Chad sat on a chair, changing dance shoes into street shoes.

In an uneasy pace, Lauren kept her hands on her hips, her stare on the door. "We were." Then she wondered if something had happened to Alex's father.

"Maybe I should call him." Chad reached for his cell phone but Lauren stopped him.

"I'll do it." Jogging over to her purse, she tugged out her cell phone, and dialed.

"You guys would make a great couple, if you ask me," he said.

Lauren's cheeks warmed. She was still getting to know Chad, so talking about her private life with him was out of the question. It was too easy for confidences to end up on a limb for the dance world to see. When Alex didn't answer his cell phone, she tapped hers to her chin, thinking.

She wondered if it would appear too eager calling him

at his mother's. Then again, if he wasn't there, he might not appreciate a strange woman calling and alerting his mother to…to what, Lauren couldn't pinpoint exactly. Did Alex's mother know about the sponsorship? Even though she had met the woman, Lauren doubted Mrs. Saunders would remember. The circumstances of their introduction had been precarious to say the least.

"He's not answering." She dialed his home. "I hope his father is all right."

Chad stood and gathered his things as if he was going to leave anyway. "Alex is a busy guy. Maybe he just got swamped." Chad headed to the door with a shrug. "There's always tomorrow. I gotta run. See ya."

So typical, Lauren thought, watching Chad. The carefree existence of the single person looked amazingly untroubled; at least that was the view from her laden shoulders.

Undeniably, she was concerned about Alex. He'd told her he would be there, and when he gave his word, he kept it. She remembered once when he'd pulled her aside by one of her bunny ears and told her he'd get her after school. The threat had scared her to death but she hadn't run. No, she'd been waiting for him right by the flagpole and when he'd stormed over, she'd been both excited and terrified.

He hadn't touched her that day, just verbally slapped her with rude comments she now realized were a boy's discomfort at confusing feelings. She smiled.

She'd been just as confused as he then, all messed up at the jumble he stirred inside of her. That mishmash of feelings had finally broken apart, leaving her with a solid knowledge that she was falling for Alex, and falling fast.

Was there really anything wrong with that? She stared

at her reflection in the mirror and doubted it. They were both consenting adults, and they had shared two extremely hot kisses. More than good-bye or even hello kisses. They'd been steaming, unforgettable, one-of-a-kind kisses. But then who was she fooling? He was a one-of-a-kind man.

Lauren danced alone, watching herself for correct movement. Dancing clarified things for her. Moving freed not only physical demons, but mental beasts sloughed away, at least as long as her body was lost in dance.

She hadn't heard the door open, nor was she aware he was there, not until she finally stopped, perspiration dampening her skin again, her breath soaring in and out. Her eyes met his across the large room, and her heart skipped.

He stood frozen, staring at her. Over his arm were slung several black garment bags.

The day had been one snag after another. Between attending to his mother's needs, his daily visit with his father and his meeting at Giant Steps, Alex had wondered if he'd ever get to the seamstress's in time to pick up Lauren and Chad's costumes and get to rehearsal. He'd counted the hours until now.

He was stunned at the sight of her and started the long walk across the room with every cell in his body jittering. He set aside the heavy costumes of beads and sequins without gentleness or care, not even glancing as he tossed them toward a chair. His gait never slowed until he was against her and had her in his arms.

Thrusting greedy hands into her hair, he angled her head so that he could more fully soak in her face. Then he smiled, and his intense grip softened, his eyes fluttering to her lips.

His mouth covered hers covetously, with all of the

passion the twenty-four hour separation dictated. Within seconds his hands left the lushness of her hair and wandered with need to far more enticing places. Down her dampened neck, along her shoulders, to the moist flesh of her arms until they slipped possessively around her waist and he brought her body tight to his.

It seemed like days since he'd seen her, yet it had been less than one. He'd missed her. Every part of him had missed her. Reluctantly he broke the firm seal of their mouths and eased back so he could look at her.

"Hey." He traced a finger along her chin, allowing it to linger on the fullness of her lower lip.

Her tongue grazed the tip of his finger. "You're late," she told him.

"I've had four days packed into one. I'm sorry."

"Is everything okay?"

Nodding, he finally loosened his arms around her. "How was your day?"

It had been so long since anyone had asked her that, she felt a rush of emotion bind her chest. "It was wonderful, actually."

"You deserve it." He led her to where the black garment bags had been abandoned on the chair. "I guess I missed Chad."

"Yes." Lauren felt the tingle of excitement start in her toes. "You brought them."

He pulled one of the bags up and held it high, unzipping it. Lauren got her first peek of deep sapphire, glittering silver, and diamonds. She gasped when he eased the dress out. It was breathtaking.

The heat from Alex's voice shuddered through her. "I

want to see you in it."

She took the dress from him and went directly to the mirror, holding it under her chin, her smile beyond pleased. "It's stunning."

Alex came up behind her and they looked at each other in the reflection. His eyes shot dark and suddenly his hands were at her waist. "Put it on."

"I'm sweaty, I don't want to ruin—"

"Put it on." Already his mouth was watering. When he'd first seen the dress, let the slick fabric crusted with sequins and jewels slink through his fingers, he'd squeezed it, the desire to see it covering her almost more than he could bear. Now she was telling him that she was too sweaty to relieve him of his mental agony?

He turned, and started toward the door. "I'll give you five minutes. Then I'm coming back in here whether you're dressed or not." The door slammed behind him.

Lauren shuddered and took in a deep breath. For a moment she was too stunned to move, then anger flashed. How dare he give her an ultimatum. She stormed toward the chairs and another shudder wove inside. She started stripping off her clothes, the thrill of his demand and her submission overriding and demolishing her anger.

The dress slipped on like a glove, settling into every curve with precision as she angled her arms to work the zipper up. The sight stopped her. She turned, admiring the perfect fit, the flash of color and light, the tease of fringe at the hem whenever she moved.

Pulse skipping she looked at the door waiting.

Only seconds passed, and Alex flung the door open. He seemed to take a minute to gather himself, and then he crossed to her, his black slacks whispering against his lean legs. She loved it when he wore all one color like tonight. Black made his image pop out with the intense drama of a hungry lover on the hunt.

"Wow." He reached out and turned her as if she were his to examine thoroughly and without question. "That's…it's… unbelievably beautiful."

Accepting his approval, she joined his appreciative assessment in the reflection of the mirror. "It really is. I've never seen anything so dazzling."

"Yes." The low engine of his voice brought her eyes to his. The nerves in her skin sprung to attention when his long, exquisite fingers trailed her bare arms. He took her hands in his and pulled her back against him, then his lips grazed the side of her neck. Ribbons of heat tingled from her neck to her toes and she flung her head back against his collarbone, closing her eyes.

His kisses seared deep into her skin, stirring everything inside of her. She turned and wrapped herself around him, looking up into his eyes. Need had her fingers pressing firmly into the back of his neck so that he would place those kisses on her mouth.

But he stopped. "Not if we want this dress to make it to competition." Gingerly he placed a very sweet, light kiss across her lips but didn't let it linger.

He was right. Between the two of them, the beautiful gown could be in shreds within seconds. Where she was no stranger to discipline, her system revved under his stealthy hands, and she wanted more from him. Sure it had been much longer for her than it had for him, she forced herself back a step.

After taking a deep breath, she turned around and they both looked at the dress again in the reflection of the mirror. "It's going to be the star of the comp," she said factually.

Alex set his hands on her shoulders. "You're going to be the star of the comp." His hands slipped down the bare skin of her arms until they fell away. "I'll let you change." The sigh in his voice had Lauren wondering if he was thinking what she was.

Coyly, she arched her back. "Could you just start the zipper for me?" In the mirror's reflection Lauren fought a grin, focusing on the way Alex' jaw knotted at the request. His gaze raked her back, his fingers twitched.

The moment his fingers made contact with the fabric, sparkling fire filled her chest shooting to her hands and legs, pooling low in her stomach. She'd pushed with the challenge. He was having his revenge now, the slow ascent of the zipper agonizing.

Involuntarily Lauren's head fell back. Like a slave to its master, her back once again pressed into him, her head dropping against his chest for more.

"Don't tempt me, Lauren."

Delicious trembling fluttered through her in a yearning that begged for his touch. Visions of his beautiful hands skimming her every inch, of what their bodies could do together there on the hard, unyielding dance floor sent her mind reeling with need for him.

"I want to tempt you," she murmured, turning her face to his. Their lips locked in naked heat, demanding what couldn't be.

His strong hands gripped her shoulders, turned her and eased her a good breathable foot away from him. Weak-kneed, still rushing with desire, she stood like a foal on its own for the first time.

"When I make love to you," Alex's voice was the kind, familiar tone of a lover, "It won't be on the dance floor, erotic as that might be."

Her hands slipped up and covered his. "I want it there." She couldn't believe she had admitted such a thing to him. Her fantasies had played with the idea, but she would have never told him. It was too personal, showing him too much of something she guarded fiercely, her private intimate thoughts.

The smile he wore told her he was pleased to know. "That's what I like about you." He reached a finger to her cheek. "You're full of surprises."

"I won't make excuses for what I want," she said, defenses creeping in. She crossed to where she had left her dancewear.

"And I wouldn't want you to." He started toward the door. "But neither do I," he opened the door, "make excuses for what I want. I just make sure I get it."

The door shut silently behind him, and a quiet pleasure echoed through Lauren and wrapped around her heart.

twenty-six

How things change, Lauren thought, hanging the dress on the back of her bedroom door. If anyone had told her a few weeks ago that she would be sponsored by Alex Saunders, developing respect and admiration, as well as a healthy desire for him, she would have laughed them in the face.

Admiring the dress, she noticed that Rebekah, too, had discovered the brilliant, flickering sequins and gems. Lauren recognized the gleam in her daughter's eyes.

"Oh, no you don't." Scooping her child in her arms, Lauren took her right to the dress and shook her head. "This is a no-no. Do not touch mommy's dress, Rebekah or...or..." Lauren wasn't sure what would work to keep her child away from the dress, and suddenly wished she had left it in Alex's care. All she needs is for Rebekah to undo a few of the delicately hand-sewn jewels and she'd look like Cinderella after the ball.

Rebekah reached for the dress in spite of Lauren's warning and Lauren knew hiding it would take great creativity, as there was no child as tenacious as hers when she got her mind set on something.

Setting Rebekah back on her feet, Lauren gently folded the dress over her arm, aware of Rebekah's eyes keenly locked on the garment.

Searching for a suitable hiding place proved impossible. Rebekah was on her tail like a thief after a diamond necklace.

"You're not going to leave this alone, are you?" Lauren sighed after her fourth attempt. With the dress still over her arm, she picked up her phone and dialed. The hot buzz that Alex's voice shot through her brought a smile to her face.

"Please tell me you miss me already," he laughed into the phone.

"Yes, I do as a matter of fact. Hey, could you do something for me?"

"Is it urgent?"

"No. I just need you to keep my dress at your place. Rebekah's taken a liking to it and I'm afraid if she gets a hold of it, I'll be wearing threads for the competition."

"You'd look fantastic in threads."

"Yes, well." She cleared her throat with a laugh. "Just come by when you can. I'll guard it with my life until then."

"I shouldn't be too long. I'm at Mother's."

"Is everything all right?"

"She just wanted me to help her move a few things around, and I wanted to see Dad."

His conscientiousness impressed her. "You're a good son, Alex," she said with all sincerity.

There was a pause on the line before he said, "I'll be there in a few."

It lifted her spirits, talking to him – being near him. Lauren realized how much she enjoyed everything about Alex. How things had changed. Laughing to herself, she carried the dress with her as Rebekah followed, entranced by the garment.

To help break her daughter's fascination, Lauren zipped the dress away in the garment bag then hung it on the inside of the bathroom door before shutting it.

"There. No more dress."

When the doorbell rang, Lauren glanced at her watch. It couldn't possibly be Alex, he was at least fifteen minutes away at the Saunders' estate.

Lauren hoisted Rebekah onto her hip and carried her to the front door, peeking out the front room window into the darkness. Her driveway was empty.

She opened the door to find Damian dressed in his work suit. A sour waft of alcohol tickled her nose. A cigarette dangled from his reckless grin.

"Hey." He dipped his head in a nod of greeting, eyes squinting with mischief. "How ya doin', Lauren?"

He reeked of alcohol, smoke and sweat. Instinct had Lauren blocking the open door with her body. Rebekah wriggled impatiently on her hip, but she didn't put her down.

"Damian."

"Was in the neighborhood, thought I'd stop by." Plucking the cigarette from his lips, he blew out a curl of smoke. "This your little girl?" He leaned in the door, inching closer.

"Yes. This is Rebekah."

"Hey, Rebekah." Cigarette between his fingers, he reached out and ruffled her hair.

Because Rebekah turned away from the smoke and was sliding from her grip, Lauren was forced to let her down. The child disappeared to the back of the house.

Lauren faced Damian, swamped with uncertainty. "So."

"Mind if I come in?" He took another step.

She took one back. "Now's not a very good time."

"Yeah. I figured."

So why are you here? she wondered silently.

He inched his shoulder into the jamb. "Alarm workin' okay?" He flicked the half-dead cigarette down to the porch and tamped it out.

"It's fine."

Shoving his hands in his front pockets, he peered in at the control pad. With one sly step, he was inside looking at it. "We mean to please."

"Well, it's running smoothly." Her heart began to pound. "Thank you."

"I want to take you out for dinner."

"You hardly look ready for a dinner date," she said lightly.

His grin spread. "I always liked that about you, that you said what was on that beautiful mind of yours. Yeah. I made a stop at the bar. As I was sitting there, I thought about you. I thought about how hot you were that night at the dance. That was a Halloween I'll never forget."

Lauren swallowed a thick knot. Nervously, her hand still held the door open. "That wasn't a pleasant night for me. I'm sure you understand why."

Damian reached out to stroke her cheek, but she moved her head aside, her expression hardening. "I think you should go."

"Come on. That was so long ago. We're all grown up now." His gaze dipped to her breasts. "We're way past that."

"I thought so too." She opened the door wider in hopes he would exit. "But you've come inside when I've made it clear that it's too late for any socializing. Don't force me to be rude, Damian. Please."

He seemed to consider what she said, his eyes slitting. Reaching out, he gripped the door with his hand and yanked it out of her grasp. Her eyes flew wide with shock. "Then don't be rude."

Too astounded for words, Lauren couldn't move, even

when he closed the door and leaned against it, still smiling at her.

"I asked you to leave."

"Simmer down, little beauty. I'm just here for a friendly visit and to check out your alarm. I can see that the alarm is working fine. Now, it's time for the visit part. I've been watching you for a while now," he said, slow as dripping molasses.

The idea sent a skittering of dread down her spine, but she stood more erect. "At the studio, of course."

He lifted a shoulder. "Here and there. Then I caught you and Alex at that competition and wondered if you two were an item. I couldn't tell." His shoulder came away from the door, and he moved closer. "It looked like you two were having a lover's quarrel. But then, sparks always flew when the two of you were near each other."

The distant sound of Rebekah's prattling took Lauren from the corner where Damian seemed intent to box her and toward her child's bedroom. Still, her heart had not slowed. With Damian following, she started weighing options.

"I need to check on Rebekah," she tossed over her shoulder at him.

"No problem."

He followed her into Rebekah's bedroom, where the child stood on her plastic bookshelf singing nonsensically with a book in her hand. Sure Damian would not do anything rash with her child present. Lauren went to Rebekah and held her.

Damian's eyes were dark under heavy lids. He leaned in the doorway. "So I called Alex. I wanted to see what was up, you know, the status between you two before I came around."

"Oh."

"You're amazing," he rolled on. "But then you know that. And that's what gets me about you. You always did act like you owned the world. Even then. Even that night." He took a step into the room.

Though her heart was flying in her chest, she knew better than to show fear. Rather than act like his barging in uninvited was unacceptable, she decided to take a deep breath and do her best to get him to leave. "You're perception of me is flattering but not accurate," she started. Rebekah squirmed free of her arms, leaving her unnervingly vulnerable. "It was nice of you to stop by, but it's too late for me to go out for something to eat. I don't have anyone that can watch Rebekah."

His brain seemed slow to comprehend what she was saying. He blinked heavily, then his eyes narrowed. "You still think you're too good for me, don't you?"

"I never thought I was too good for you." Lauren worked to keep her voice steady. "I never thought of you that way, you know that."

The corner of his lip lifted. "'Cause you were always chasing after Alex."

"I never chased after Alex. He hated me, or have you forgotten?"

"I haven't forgotten anything about you." He took a slow, deliberate step in her direction. "Your skin, the way you breathe. The perfume you wore. The way you felt underneath me."

"I really think you should go now." Panic rose from her stomach. Over by the window, Rebekah was climbing on a chair, her little fingers working on the lock. "I need to stop her—"

"Come on, Lauren." The musty scent of his workday

filled her head when he stepped close. One arm reached out, his fingers wrapping around her bicep. Fear froze her. He licked his lips before pulling her against him, his focus on her mouth.

"Damian, I need to stop Rebekah, she's—"

Damian glanced at the child to see what she was doing and Lauren stole the momentary lapse in his grip to dart over and stand between Damian and Rebekah. She hoped he would have the sense not to do anything stupid. Lauren ignored her pounding heart, took Rebekah by the hand and headed out the bedroom door.

"It's getting late." A shiver tickled her spine when he shadowed her hasty exit, his sour breath on her neck. "I need to get her to bed."

"Oh. Sure," he said. "How about another night?"

Lauren let out a sigh of relief. This was almost over. Rebekah squirmed and reached for her bedroom as Lauren took her down the hall. "No." Lauren's grip tightened. "You're staying with Mommy."

"She's feisty, just like her momma." Damian's grin spread. "Aren't you, baby?"

Catching a glance at her watch, Lauren prayed Alex would be arriving soon. That would deflect any unwanted overtures from Damian. If he didn't show up, well, she tried to plan her alternatives.

Rebekah finally wriggled down, and she ran into the kitchen. Lauren was quick to follow. "You can see yourself out," she told him, but he kept right behind her.

Rebekah went to the bowl of fruit sitting on top of the counter and plucked an orange. "Orng…orng…orng…"

"She loves oranges," Lauren said in hopes of changing the subject and lightening tension. Rebekah sat, running her fingers along her palm with a glassy stare into nowhere while she waited. With shaky hands, Lauren cut the orange into chunks. After she'd placed the cut fruit in front of Rebekah, she crossed to the sink to wash her hands. She kept the knife in her hand as she rinsed it.

Damian started toward her. "She knows what's good."

Lauren turned off the water, keeping a hold of the paring knife. "She thinks she can cut it all by herself." Holding the knife conspicuously, Lauren faced him. "Of course... I don't let her."

Damian glanced down at the knife and stopped in his tracks. "That would be... dangerous."

Lauren felt undeniably better holding the blade. "Maybe you should go now."

Damian's eyes slit. "Maybe I will, after we settle on a date."

"It would be a waste of your time." The fervor with which he was looking at her left her only one option. "I'm seeing someone."

Disappointment mixed with amusement on his face. "Damn. It's Saunders, isn't it?"

Lauren nodded.

He let out a laugh. "Well, that ought to make him happy. He's been dying to get under that bunny tail of yours for as long—"

"Now you're being crude." Lauren took a step toward him, brandishing the knife. "I think it's time for you to leave."

With a sarcastic snort, Damian cocked his head.

The knock on the door was the most wonderful sound Lauren had heard all night. Quickly, she crossed the kitchen, went through the door and headed for the living room, opening the front door with a wide, relieved smile.

"Alex."

His smile of pleasure met hers. Then he saw Damian.

Lauren stood back so Alex could enter and he came right in, fitting himself firmly between her and Damian.

Damian stuck out his hand with a crooked smile. "What's up, man?"

"A little late to be making service calls, isn't it?" Alex glanced at the extended hand while his own twitched at his sides.

"Not here about the alarm," Damian said. "I came by to ask this lovely lady to dinner."

Alex looked at Lauren. Her wide eyes and the knife she held brought suspicion to his heart, though he fought ignoring it with the appearance of cordiality. "Did I come at a bad time, then?"

"No," she said. It brought a glimmer of satisfaction to Alex when she laid her hand on his arm. He held her frantic gaze with silent reprimand. "He was just leaving actually."

"Unfortunately, she's turned me down." Damian eyed Alex, eyed the way Lauren's hand lingered on his arm.

"Then I guess it's time for you to say goodbye." Blocking Lauren with his body, Alex held the door open in blunt invitation for Damian to exit.

Damian started for the door. "Lauren." He nodded at her as he passed.

After Damian had gone through the door, Alex turned to Lauren. "I'll be right back."

"Where are you going?"

He didn't say anything, just followed Damian. Lauren waited in the doorway, watching the two men dissolve in the shadows of her front yard.

Alex's fists flexed. He was so ready to whip Damian around and slam him into the nearest tree he could barely control his contempt. His fuse had always been short, and he'd spent the most recent years of his life working to control the violent craving.

"Buddy," he called out. Damian stopped and turned. Darkness thickened as shadows and moonlight fought for dominance. "You hanging around for a reason?"

Damian shrugged. "That's obvious, isn't it?"

"She's told you to get lost, what, twice now?' Alex shook his head with a laugh meant to bite. "In anybody's book, that would mean move on."

Damian stuck a cigarette between his teeth. "Yeah, well, I'm not anybody."

Alex stepped closer, his body tight. "She's mine."

Even with their noses nearly touching, Damian lit the cigarette, and promptly blew smoke in Alex's face before he let out a snarling laugh. "That's what she said." When Alex's face flashed with confusion, Damian didn't laugh, rather his eyes slit over a smile. "Looks like you two have some things to talk about."

"It won't be you."

Spitting out a laugh, Damian looked back at the house. "No, I'm guessing I'm too late for that." His dark eyes narrowed on Alex.

"Thought you gave up drinking." Alex exaggerated a disproving sniff.

"Yeah, well, not all of us can drown our losses in the woman of our dreams." Damian sucked in a long breath and held it. "You haven't lost your touch my friend."When Lauren opened the door they both looked over. She remained in the jamb, watching.

"He's leaving," Alex said.

Damian sent Lauren one last grin. "Be flattered, Lauren. Be very flattered." Backing away, he saluted her before strolling out of sight.

Alex's dark eyes flashed when he passed her in the door.

"Two grown men fighting like school boys in my front yard."

Once he'd shut the door, Alex reached out and swung her around. "You want him here? In your life?"

"Of course not." She pulled free and continued into the kitchen. Rebekah was standing on the end of the kitchen table, rubbing her palm with her fingers, singing light mutterings. Lauren went to her and hefted her to her hip before facing Alex again.

"I was just as surprised as you when he came by."

"He was under the impression that you wanted him around."

"Well, he's delusional," Lauren said. Damian's visit had been unsettling to say the least. "I told him it was too late, but he came right on in."

"For hell's sake, Lauren, why did you open the door?"

"I thought it might be you!" Her voice rose. "And I didn't see his car in the driveway. Don't get on me for something I didn't do." Rebekah squealed and squirmed, their raising voices setting her system on alert. It was no use to try and restrain her. Lauren had to let her go. The child darted out of the room.

"He's dangerous." Alex blocked her from following Rebekah. Looking down into her eyes, the hard lines in his face started to soften some. "What if I hadn't gotten here when I did?"

That was all it took to soften her as well. Her shoulders slumped forward on a wispy sigh. "I'm glad you came when you did, Alex." Laying her hand on his arm, she took note of the fierce protective flicker in his eyes.

Alex set his hands on her shoulders, his gaze sweeping her from head to toe. He would know no peace until she was his. He was more than ready to make her his own, but judged the timing too soon. His would be a challenge of creating an even balance as he continued to pursue and protect her without her knowing it.

"You look peaked. Did something happen?"

She knew what would happen if she told him Damian had tried to kiss her. He'd be out the door hunting him down, and she was enjoying the comfort of having him there too much. "Nothing."

"Lauren, I want the truth."

"I took care of it." It felt good to curl her fingers around his wrists, to feel his blood pulse hard for her.

"He said something," Alex started, wondering if he'd imagined Damian's words.

"What?"

"That...never mind. You sure you're all right?"

Lauren nodded. It would be easy to dive into him at that moment, wrapping her arms around him, burying her head in the firm strength of his chest to listen to his heart beat. She liked that she could rest her head against something real. Why did she feel guilty, wanting that?

She was a woman, attracted to a man she had convinced herself was off limits. But he wanted her, she knew that as definitely as she knew every step of waltz, or cha-cha, or samba. As well as she knew denying the truth in her heart any longer would be futile.

The thought of dance brought to her mind the dress, and Alex's reason for being there. Panicked, she raced to the bathroom. When she saw the bathroom light on, the door slightly ajar, her stomach flipped.

The bathroom was empty and Lauren whirled around, bumping into Alex in the doorway. "She's got the dress," she said, moving around him.

They found Rebekah sitting in the corner of Lauren's bedroom, the dress haphazardly pulled over her body. Fingering the delicately swirling patterns of sequins and jewels, Rebekah looked up through big, blue eyes when Lauren and Alex entered.

Lauren stopped in the door, her heart in the clutch of surprise. She pressed her hand across her mouth in amazement.

Noticing her expression, Alex put an arm around her. "What is it?"

"She—" Lauren could barely believe the sight before her eyes, and started laughing as tears rolled down her cheeks. "She's never dressed herself before." Going to Rebekah's side, she sunk to her knees, enveloping the wide-eyed child against her breast. "Baby. You got yourself dressed. Good job." She looked up at Alex through teary eyes. "I never thought she'd be able to figure it out and look at her – in one of my dresses."

Lowering next to her, Alex smiled into Rebekah's face. "That's great news."

"I can't believe it." Lauren rocked a squirming Rebekah in her arms. "I know it sounds like nothing, but it really is huge news." She kissed Rebekah on the cheek before standing her up. "But now it's time to take off Mommy's dress, pretty girl."

Rebekah squealed with refusal and tried to dart away, but Alex's strong arms were there to catch her, and he brought her against him in a confident, non-threatening hug. Lauren admired the site of her child safely tucked in Alex's capable arms. An involuntary breath whispered out of her lungs.

"Mommy wants her dress now, Rebekah. Let's take it off for her." Carefully, Alex held Rebekah as Lauren started easing the delicate fabric down her little body. Rebekah whined in protest, her lips turning into a pout.

"She's a firecracker, isn't she?" Without Alex's patient hands, Lauren doubted she would have gotten the dress off in one piece. As Alex lifted Rebekah, Lauren slipped the dress out from underneath her and stood. Letting it ripple free she checked for damage. Finding none, she hung it back on the wooden hangar and carefully placed it inside the garment bag.

When she'd finished, she turned. Alex stood with Rebekah in his arms, the two of them staring at each other. Alex was quietly talking, and the hushed movement of his lips held Rebekah's fascination.

"You're very pretty," his voice was light and wispy, and Rebekah's round blue eyes shifted from his lips to his eyes. "Very pretty like mommy," he added. Then he kissed her cheek before his gaze swept around for Lauren.

The moment was silent, stretching like the delicate, glimmering fabric of the dress Lauren would wear against her body. Fabric Alex had designed with her curves, her shape and her skin in mind. A hot rush of admiration flowed through her for him, drawing from her an involuntary breath. She licked her lips.

She liked that he watched. Slowly, he eased Rebekah
to the floor, his dark eyes locked on her, causing her heart
to thud. Rebekah ran right to the garment bag and started
unzipping it.

Frazzled by the intense vibe thickening the air around
them, Lauren scooped Rebekah into her arms with a flustered
blush. "Let me put her to bed." She passed him, inhaling his
scent, lighting her desire to a voracious flame.

Usually, she read Rebekah a story, lay in bed with her
and tried to cuddle before putting her down for the night. But
her blood was too hot, and tonight it raced through her veins
like the quickstep.

Washing Rebekah's hands and face, she looked at her
own in the reflection of the mirror and realized she desperately
needed some blush. Trying to brush Rebekah's teeth was like
pulling a tooth without Novocain, and for tonight, Lauren
decided the battle could wait.

She helped Rebekah change into pajamas, kneeled with
her at her bedside for prayer and then tucked her into bed.
Rebekah's wide eyes told Lauren she might be out of luck
for any uninterrupted romance. Sleep looked as far out of
Rebekah's reach as Alex did for Lauren.

But she wouldn't give up that easily, she told herself
closing Rebekah's door. "'Night, pretty girl." There was no
reply, but with Alex somewhere in her house, the silence didn't
sting as much. She had witnessed a miracle tonight. Rebekah
had dressed herself, what more could she ask for?

He stood near the front door, as if ready to leave.
Lauren's ripe heart sunk.

"You're leaving?" she asked.

He held the dress over his arm and patted it gently with

a nod. Hadn't he been sucked into the heat like she had? What was this control, this white-iron strength he was exuding while she was turning to lusty mush?

She crossed her arms, tilting her head at him. "I thought you never backed away from a challenge."

"I don't." The brown in his eyes turned black. "The dress is safe. If I don't leave now, neither one of us will be."

She crossed to him, slow and easy, and enjoyed the way his face drew taut. "Since when did either of us run from danger?"

The muscles in his throat constricted as he struggled with what to say. It sent a fast, sharp thrill of satisfaction through her.

Without warning, he tossed the garment bag aside and snatched her. His body, hard and hot, demanded she own up to the taunt she'd so recklessly teased him with. Possessively, he wrapped one arm around her waist, the other fisted in her hair before bringing her face under his.

Black fury lit his eyes, stirring her deep inside. Willingly, she melded into him. Her lips strained for his but he only burned them with his ravenous gaze. "I want more than this, Lauren." The rasp of his voice drove into her core. "I've always wanted more from you."

"What more do you want?" Her own voice scraped with need. Her arms wound around his neck. There had never been anything like this, and Lauren knew he was the only man she would feel this way for. The only man that could make her pride both prickle and dissolve.

He looked at her with disbelief, as if she didn't understand the depth of what he was asking. "I don't want to share you with anyone. Ever. That's what I want."

A grin spread her lips wide. "I like that you're possessive."

"You would. It drives me crazy to see any man even looking at you." Urgency intensified in his eyes. "And I could kill any that want to touch you." It was then that he smothered her mouth with his.

Gentleness was discarded for greed. Patience abandoned for satiety. She couldn't breathe; his arms squeezed her heart into her ribs, and it strained to unite with his.

His lips pulled from hers and traveled along her cheek to her ear where he nipped the soft flesh of her lobe. "I don't think I can wait any longer."

If she waited, she wouldn't be alive in the morning, she decided, cupping the taut lines of his jaw in her hands. Ferocious need scored his face in torment and agony she knew only she could ease. The power lit her insides with a flame that would not be extinguished by anything other than consummated love.

Her hands slid from the tense corners of his face, down his neck and shoulders, finally taking his hands in hers.

He didn't say anything, rather scooped her into his arms and carried her down the hall to her bedroom. Her nerves spun, whirling like a dancer soaring out of control.

twenty-seven

He kicked her bedroom door open. It sent Lauren's body into another delicious jolt of anticipation. Though he'd been forceful with the door, he laid her on her bed with the care of the most fragile long-stemmed rose. Then he stood back.

"I want to look at you," he said. "Just look."

Her heart hammered. She couldn't slow her ragged breath if she tried. His eyes darkened with such intensity, she felt branded by his ownership, leeched of will, leaving complete submission.

Lauren's heart slowed, finding a steady, fervent beat driven by love and admiration. To be accepted and wanted was something she had yearned for. Lust was fleeting, that she knew. Her body shifted from hot and hungry to something much more penetrating and lasting.

She held out her hand to him and he took it. Gently, she pulled him toward her. With care he knelt next to the side of the bed. The virtuous gesture caused her soul to open.

"I love you, Lauren."

The words were barely a whisper, but they drove into her heart with such force, Lauren's breath held in her chest. She wanted him. No one but him. Shifting to her side, she reached out and stroked his cheek.

The warm silence was broken only by the faint sounds of Rebekah's melodic voice across the hall. Lauren swallowed disbelief. Moments ago they had made it clear they wanted each other. Dare she really think he meant it? His intense gaze confirmed her fragile concerns were unfounded.

As if another door had been kicked open, her heart flew to freedom. She felt a smile, tears, and excruciating relief all at once. "I love you, too."

She had never seen such reprieve. The taut planes of his face relaxed, pulling back into a glorious smile. He leaned close, his head dipped as if to kiss but he merely teased with nearness. Tenderly, he brushed the hair back from her face, content to gaze upon her.

"Kiss me," she whispered.

"Only if you'll marry me."

She froze. Her wide eyes locked with his.

Alex's heart stopped beating. He wanted her, but he wouldn't give her any more of himself until he had her heart. Anything less would take what he had prized and held out for and make it equal to every other woman he'd had a relationship with. Lauren would never be like any other woman.

She blinked fast, uncertainty in her eyes. He fought the urge to protect his heart and ego by pulling away and brushed a light kiss across her lips. He meant to lure the answer from her by reminding her of the electricity their bodies and souls had felt since that first day so many years ago.

She whispered, "Only you would attach an offer of marriage to—"

"Because that's how I want it with you. I want the ultimate surrender, the most complete gift."

"Will it always be like this?" Her voice was soft. "You and I butting heads about everything, even whether or not I say yes to you?"

He rested on his elbows then, bringing her hands, still in his, next to his heart. His smile grew, gleaming in the soft lamplight. "I hope so."

"Then I'll most definitely marry you." Tingling, Lauren watched his lips slowly come to hers.

His taste filled her, shooting through her senses like an intoxicating spice. She slid closer and wrapped her arms around his neck, inviting him up from his knees, but he didn't move.

His voice was raw between kisses. "My way, Lauren."

Confusion was quickly replaced by respect. Holding his face cupped in her hands, she admired the firm determination there.

"I want you wearing my ring."

"I don't need your ring," she was nearly delirious, heart banging, head swimming. The heat of his lips fluttered torturously slow across the pulsing urgency in her mouth.

"I want to see it on your hand when we're making love." Trailing kisses along her jaw, to her chin, Alex's lips spoke against hers. "To know that you're bound to me."

His eyes met hers and held. Surrender would never be more frightening, thrilling or complete.

A loud crash froze them both. Alex was off of his knees in a breath, and pulling Lauren upward. They rushed together to Rebekah's door, but it was Lauren that flung it open.

The bookshelf laid flat, Rebekah stunned and dazed, underneath it. Her blue eyes met Lauren's and Lauren's heart skipped a beat.

Lauren rushed to her side. "Baby?" The second Alex lifted the shelf, Lauren pulled Rebekah into her arms. "Honey, are you okay?" Lauren rocked her back and forth, but Rebekah just blinked hard and stuck her thumb in her mouth.

Gently Alex ran his hand against Rebekah's head. "She's not crying."

"Sometimes pain doesn't register quickly for her."

"Kind of a delayed reaction then?"

"She probably won't cry. It's just not something she does unless she's really hurt or unhappy."

Assessing the plastic bookshelf, Alex doubted the shelf itself had hurt her. But the fall might have. "Lauren, if she fell from the top of it, she may need to be checked. You want to take her in?"

"She hates the doctor. Being touched, examined…she'll throw a fit." Lauren hated that Alex would see just how difficult a visit to the doctor could be. Something inside of her worried that he might decide she and her daughter were too much baggage for someone already overloaded by his own family.

"Let's take her in just to be sure." His gentle touch was at her back and Lauren found herself willingly escorted out the door. He grabbed her purse, Rebekah's coat, and soon they were sitting like a family in his warm car

Rebekah sat strapped in the back seat, sucking her thumb in silence. Swamped with gratitude, choked with fear that Alex would be turned off by what she knew lay ahead, Lauren kept her gaze out the window. Until she felt his warm hand rest on her thigh, palm upward, waiting for hers. She set her hand in his.

"It's going to get ugly at the hospital," she murmured.

"We'll take care of it."

"She hates it. I mean she really hates it. They'll have to hold her down. She'll scream—"

"Lauren." His dark eyes held hers across the dimly lit front seat. "It will be all right. You're not going to do this alone…not tonight, not ever again." When he squeezed her hand, she let out an involuntary breath.

* * *

Two hours later, Alex carried an exhausted Rebekah out, cradled in his arms. It amazed him that a little body could fit submissively against him, when just hours earlier that same little body had kicked, screamed and fought, controlled by an untamed will.

It had been hard to watch the team of doctors and nurses work in a frenzy to hold the child still so they could make sure nothing was wrong. He didn't know how many children with autism went to the ER, but judging from the perplexed looks on the doctors and nurses faces, he doubted they had seen many.

Alex's heart had ached watching what the struggle had done to Lauren. Steadfastly she'd kept physical contact with her writhing, hysterical child as any mother would. The tear that slipped unnoticed down her cheek by the busy physicians had brought a thick knot to his throat. In the end, Rebekah had been without anything more than a few bruises.

Alex strapped Rebekah into her car seat, hoping not to awaken her. Her little face was puffy and red from the extreme exertion. Her eyes remained closed, her head rolled to the side in sleep.

He let out a breath.

When he stood upright, he found Lauren next to him, her eyes glistening under the night's hazy moon. "Thank you." Her voice trembled out.

He wrapped his arms around her, feeling complete when she melded into the strength and support he meant to give her. "Let's get you two home."

Without another word he drove, his mind heavy with his life, her life, and how the two would fit together. Her silence had him wondering if the events of the evening had, in her mind, diluted what had happened between them before Rebekah's fall. He hoped she didn't think that he'd been scared off.

When they arrived back at Lauren's, he carried Rebekah to her bedroom, then waited while Lauren made sure she was safely tucked in for the rest of the night. When she finally joined him in the hall, he saw the weary warrior he'd seen weeks ago when Rebekah had run away. He wondered how many of her days ended like this.

Without hesitation she went directly into his arms. That male part of him designed to protect and provide pulled hard deep inside. His heart tumbled in his chest. How he wanted to stay. To take her back to the bedroom and just lie with her, his body protecting, surrounding and comforting hers.

The deep sigh she let out against his chest almost undid him. His knees weakened before he locked them. Scooping her into his arms, he began another trek to her bedroom. Her arms wrapped like silk around his neck, her head burrowed under his chin.

"Stay," she whispered, sending fevered heat into his belly.

He balanced her against his thigh and flung back the covers of her bed, exposing baby pink flannel sheets. Her scent, clean and floral, came at him like a delicately blown kiss. Gently, he laid her on the bed, pushing back need, desire and longing. His hands slid down her legs and eased off her shoes. Though yearning brightened her blue eyes, he tenderly pulled the blankets up and tucked them around her. Instantly, her lids grew heavy.

Leaning over her, he caged her in. "Good night, Lauren." With care he stroked her head and placed another kiss on her still lips before she closed her eyes.

twenty-eight

Lauren awoke to Rebekah's soft murmurings drifting from behind her closed bedroom door. A dreamy smile spread across her lips. Twined with her child's ethereal sounds were thoughts of Alex and the previous night. He'd asked her to marry him.

And she'd agreed.

Lauren blinked. Covering her face with her hands she let out a fluttering laugh. The thought of marrying Alex filled her with the giddiness of a girl on her sixteenth birthday, primed for life, eager for the promises of what lie ahead.

She pulled back the blankets and remembered that she hadn't changed into her pajamas the night before. Alex had taken off her shoes and tucked her in. He'd taken care of her.

She made the bed with her mind in a dreamy haze, and went unlock Rebekah's bedroom door. She'd wanted him to stay. Retrospect had her feeling relieved they hadn't made love. She'd been emotionally stretched yesterday and hadn't been in any condition to give herself to him the way she wanted.

Rebekah was on the bookshelf when Lauren opened the door and Lauren's heart took another dip. It was then Lauren realized the bookshelf would have to go, until Rebekah's fascination with it died. Or they would go through this climbing obsession indefinitely.

"Hey, pretty girl." Lauren took her into her arms and kissed her cheek. She thought of Alex, of how he'd held Rebekah with the familiarity of a father. Not once during the uncomfortable events in the ER did she see him look at

Rebekah as anything less than a child in need of help and comfort and love.

"What do you want for breakfast?" Lauren carried Rebekah on her hip into the kitchen.

"Bfst," Rebekah said.

"Good using your words. Good asking Momma for breakfast." Lauren let Rebekah slip down her hip. "Sit at the table, please." Rebekah went right to the table and sat.

"Do you want cereal or waffles?" Lauren went to the freezer, anticipating her child's answer.

"Wffl."

Lauren dropped two of the frozen specialty waffles into her toaster. Again her mind drifted to Alex. She took in a deep breath, easily recalling the masculine scent of him, his taste. She could go without breakfast, she decided, just thinking about him was all she needed. It was as if he had left part of himself there in her house just to tantalize her.

Rebekah's waffles popped up, snapping Lauren's thoughts to the present, but the smile on her face refused to leave. She placed the waffles on a plate and poured a scant amount of maple syrup over them.

"That looks good."

Alex's voice nearly startled the plate out of her hand. He stood in the doorway with both hands in the jamb. His dark hair was a mess of naps and tangles. His shirt was unbuttoned, exposing the carved lines of his chest and the nicked shadow of his navel. Wrinkled beyond repair, he'd left the shirt hanging out of his black slacks.

He was barefoot.

"You invited me to stay." He came toward her and the move made her heart jump. She wanted to make him breakfast and give him a morning kiss this morning and every morning thereafter.

Setting the plate of waffles in front of Rebekah, Lauren forced her breath to slow down. As striking as he looked, as wifely as she felt, Rebekah was awake and the routine of getting her off to school took priority.

"And I'm glad you stayed." She cut the waffles into bite-sized pieces. Finished, she looked at him. Near enough that she could take him in with a single breath, she reached out as his arms slid around her waist. Her bones nearly melted when their bodies fused. Lauren decided she could stay right there the rest of the day, just being held.

She closed her eyes, listening to the pound of his heart beneath her ear. A slight tug at her chin turned her face up to his.

"Good morning."

She liked that his voice rasped. Running through her mind were countless fantasy mornings she could spend with him expressing good morning the way she wanted. Lifting to her toes, she kissed him. "Morning."

Rebekah's soft babblings dragged Alex's attention to the table. "Hey, Rebekah."

Staring off into nothing, Rebekah continued to eat and chatter as if no words had been spoken. Only one waffle remained.

"Where did you sleep?" Curious, Lauren eased from Alex's arms and peered into the living room where her couch still held the imprint of his body. "I hope it was comfortable. I've never slept on it."

"It was fine, as couches go." When he stretched Lauren got an eyeful of lower belly.

"Been on a lot of couches, have we?" She lifted her brow as she crossed to the refrigerator.

He let out a rumbling laugh that stirred something deep inside of her. She reached for icy orange juice. "Want some?" she asked.

"Sure." He helped himself to her cupboards in search of a small glass.

"I like the way you look here," she told him, taking a moment to enjoy the sight.

"I like the way I feel here." He set two glasses on the counter with a grin.

They decided that he would make French toast while she readied Rebekah for school. Lauren's hands shook as she dressed her child. Having Alex in her home, making breakfast was so domestically delicious; she couldn't keep from feeling like she might burst from the inside out.

Rebekah's hair was fine as shredded silk and Lauren pulled it back into a ponytail, catching her first glimpse of herself in the mirror. Her eyes shot wide. She looked like a strong wind had just blown through her. Last night's mascara smudged sooty underneath both eyes and her rouge had traveled to her ear lobes.

Aghast, she washed her face, pulled her hair on top of her head, and changed into some fresh jeans and a tee shirt. He's seen me at my best and my worst, she thought spraying a wisp of perfume at the back of her neck, then down her shirt between her breasts. And he didn't run screaming. That was feeling comfortable.

When they stood together on the front lawn and both waved goodbye as Rebekah's bus pulled away, Lauren knew she would enjoy getting used to the forgotten delight that was being married and having a companion.

They would be alone inside, and Lauren felt the heat of him next to her as they took the stairs to her front door side-by-side. He slipped his hand in hers.

He stopped at the front door, and faced her. Then brought her hand to his lips and brushed a kiss across her knuckles. "The stores open at ten, I want to go right out and take care of the ring."

The reality of what she had committed to felt like a mink coat that had been carefully placed around her shoulders. Beautiful, comforting, but so unbelievable she wasn't sure it might get snatched before she'd had a chance to enjoy it. Make it hers.

He led her inside, then sat on the couch and slipped on his socks and shoes, his brown eyes staying with her. "Does that sound good to you as a day plan?" He stood, and started buttoning his shirt.

Lauren stole the last glimpses of his chest that she could, watching the smooth skin disappear behind tricky fingers and silky fabric. "Sounds perfect."

In two strides he was flush with her, and his arms wove tight around her waist. He tugged her chin up and gazed down at her. "I like it when you watch me."

"Good, because I like to watch you."

His mouth covered hers in fresh heat, his grip drew her last breath from her lungs. Then he was out the door, leaving her a smile and his scent, and with love roving delightfully in her heart.

* * *

Glittering red spun crimson light through the room. Flashes of color from Lauren's dress sparkled into the faces of the judges, the audience, and Alex.

Whispers hushed every voice. Curiosity turned every head. Awe fastened all eyes on the stunning couple now standing front and center on the dance floor. From the edge, Alex watched with glowing pleasure at the center table.

There was no sound now but Alex's heart, thudding in his chest.

He couldn't wait to watch her move. Sitting forward, he rested his elbows on the table, his chin set in clasped fingers. His proud gaze locked on her face.

Guitars strummed, and so did Alex's nerves. She wasn't nervous, that much he knew. She'd won the competition, and this dance was merely a celebration of that win, an encore performance to satiate the enthusiastic crowd. When she didn't look over, it didn't bother him. She was performing, and theatrics demanded that she share her smile with everyone in the room.

Her hips swung slow, torturously, meting seduction in easy, captivating turns that showcased her skill, her body, and the dress that garnished both of those in sapphire intensity. Like a flickering blue flame, she moved next to Chad as he tried to possess her in the dance.

Alex didn't feel his eyes narrow, but that familiar possessiveness jagged through him hot, alive and fierce. He was learning to share her with Chad, with judges, with awe-struck audiences, with her students. Love had enabled him to open his heart completely and share her with her child.

The sparkling diamond on her finger shot its own dazzling light now, a warning and a symbol that she was taken, that she belonged to him. Alex took infinite pleasure seeing that radiance when her arm beckoned, floated and fluttered in the dance.

He swallowed a hard knot when her body rolled from toe to head like a shuddering blaze in perfect harmony with Chad's. Dance was an illusion, a beautiful, sensual fantasy, one that he was learning himself. Competing would not be necessary. No, just being able to move with her that way would be enough. Private dances were what mattered most to Alex.

When the performance was over, the audience stood in applause. And Alex rose to his feet with them. Immediately, her eyes shot to his and locked in a secret glimmering meant just for him. His insides stormed with fire. Then she was lost as the floor filled with well-wishers, dancers and judges, all clamoring to congratulate the championship couple. Alex kept his eye on her through the shifting crowd.

He lifted the two-dozen red and white roses into his arms and waited for her to come to him. Deep inside, he searched for that hole, that empty gnaw he'd harbored since he had first laid eyes on her in his youth. As if this were nothing more than the dance he had just witnessed, a dream, a fantasy that would vanish, taking with it his love for her when the music ended. But the emptiness wasn't there anymore. Their union had finally sealed that gap, and a peaceful sigh escaped him.

Her voice reached out over the excited clamoring, even over the music, now starting again. He looked for her face, and found her drawing near.

The announcer boomed through speakers, "Thank you to our champions, Chad Evans and Lauren Saunders for that encore dance. And now, we'll have some open dancing."

Alex's heart leapt when he heard her name – *his* name. It wasn't a dream, it was real. She was his.

Finally, she made it to the table. He extended his arms, overflowing with roses. "You were amazing," he said, and leaned over for a kiss.

She tantalized him by grazing her lips across his just long enough to whet his appetite. When she took the flowers, he gripped her elbow. "You're teasing me," he whispered in her ear. He liked the way she smelled after a long, hot dance – faded perfume and spent woman.

"Of course." She grinned and set the roses down next to her trophy on their table. Then she took both of his hands in hers and backed toward the bubbling dance floor, her eyes alight with mischief.

"Dance with me," she said.

Sliding his arms around her waist, he smiled down into her face. He thought she would never ask.

about the author

Katherine Warwick specializes in writing women's romance with ballroom dance as an integral part of the story. She is the mother of six children, one of whom has autism. She lives in Utah.

For more information on Katherine
and her other novels, visit her websites:
www.katherinewarwick.com   &   www.ballroomdancenovels.com

Printed in the United States
55659LVS00009BA/2

9 781933 963983